Robert Bridges

Eros and Psyche

Robert Bridges

Eros and Psyche

ISBN/EAN: 9783337076795

Printed in Europe, USA, Canada, Australia, Japan

Cover: Foto ©Andreas Hilbeck / pixelio.de

More available books at **www.hansebooks.com**

EROS & PSYCHE

BY

ROBERT BRIDGES

LONDON

GEORGE BELL AND SONS

1894

NOTE

THIS poem was first published in 1885. It has now been revised throughout, and parts of the first and second cantos rewritten. It is printed in the form originally intended, the divisions corresponding to seasons, months and days. At the end of the volume a note will be found explaining the spelling.

R. B.

YATTENDON,

1894.

FIRST QUARTER
𝕾pring

*Psyche's earthly parentage. Worshipped by men
and persecuted by Aphrodite, she is loved
and carried off by Eros.*

EROS & PSYCHE

MARCH

1

IN midmost length of hundred-citied Crete,
  The land that cradl'd Zeus, of old renown,
Where grave Demeter nurseried her wheat,
And Minos fashion'd law, ere he went down
To judge the quaking hordes of Hell's domain,
There dwelt a King on the Omphalian plain
Eastward of Ida, in a little town.

2

Three daughters had this King, of whom my tale
Time hath preserved, that loveth to despise
The wealth which men misdeem of much avail,
Their glories for themselves that they devise;
For clerkly is he, old hard-featured Time,
And poets' fabl'd song, and lovers' rhyme
He storeth on his shelves to please his eyes.

3

These three princesses all were fairest fair;
And of the elder twain 'tis truth to say
That if they stood not high above compare,
Yet in their prime they bore the palm away;
Outwards of loveliness; but Nature's mood,
Gracious to make, had grudgingly endued
And marr'd by gifting ill the beauteous clay.

4

And being in honour they were well content
To feed on lovers' looks and courtly smiles,
To hang their necks with jewel'd ornament,
And gold, that vanity in vain beguiles,
And live in gaze, and take their praise for due,
To be the fairest maidens then to view
Within the shores of Greece and all her isles.

5

But of that youngest one, the third princess,
There is no likeness; since she was as far
From pictured beauty as is ugliness,

Though on the side where heavenly wonders are,
Ideals out of being and above,
Which music worshipeth, but if love love,
'Tis, as the poet saith, to love a star.

6

Her vision rather drave from passion's heart
What earthly soil it had afore possest;
Since to man's purer unsubstantial part
The brightness of her presence was addrest:
And such as mock'd at God, when once they saw
Her heavenly glance were humbl'd, and in awe
Of things unseen, return'd to praise the Best.

7

And so before her, wheresoe'er she went,
Hushing the crowd a thrilling whisper ran,
And silent heads were reverently bent;
Till from the people the belief began
That Love's own mother had come down on earth,
Sweet Cytherea, or of mortal birth
A greater Goddess was vouchsaf't to man.

8

Then Aphrodite's statue in its place
Stood without worshippers; if Cretans pray'd
For beauty or for children, love or grace,
The prayer and vow were offer'd to the maid;
Unto the maid their hymns of praise were sung,
Their victims bled for her, for her they hung
Garland and golden gift, and none forbade.

9

And thence opinion spread beyond the shores,
From isle to isle the wonder flew, it came
Across the Ægæan on a thousand oars,
Athens and Smyrna caught the virgin's fame;
And East or West, where'er the tale had been,
The adoration of the foam-born queen
Fell to neglect, and men forgot her name.

10

No longer to high Paphos now 'twas sail'd;
The fragrant altar by the Graces served
At Cnidus was forsaken; pilgrims fail'd

The rocky island to her name reserved,
Proud Ephyra, and Meropis renown'd;
'Twas all for Crete her votaries were bound,
And to the Cretan maid her worship swerved.

11

Which when in heaven great Aphrodite saw,
Who is the breather of the year's bright morn,
Fount of desire and beauty without flaw,
Herself the life that doth the world adorn;
Seeing that without her generative might
Nothing can spring upon the shores of light,
Nor any bud of joy or love be born;

12

She, when she saw the insult, did not hide
Her indignation, that a mortal frail
With her eterne divinity had vied,
Her fair Hellenic empire to assail,
For which she had fled the doom of Ninus old,
And left her wanton images unsoul'd
In Babylon and Zidon soon to fail.

13

"Not long," she cried, "shall that poor girl of Crete
God it in my despite; for I will bring
Such mischief on the sickly counterfeit
As soon shall cure her tribe of worshipping:
Her beauty will I mock with loathèd lust,
Bow down her dainty spirit to the dust,
And leave her long alive to feel the sting."

14

With that she calls to her her comely boy,
The limber scion of the God of War,
The fruit adulterous, which for man's annoy
To that fierce partner Cytherea bore,
Eros, the ever young, who only grew
In mischief, and was Cupid named anew
In westering aftertime of latin lore.

15

What the first dawn of manhood is, the hour
When beauty, from its fleshy bud unpent,
Flaunts like the corol of a summer flower,

As if all life were for that ornament;
Such Eros seemed in years, a trifler gay,
The prodigal of an immortal day
For ever spending, and yet never spent.

16

His skin is brilliant with the nimble flood
Of ichor, that comes dancing from his heart,
Lively as fire, and redder than the blood,
And maketh in his eyes small flashes dart,
And curleth his hair golden, and distilleth
Honey on his tongue, and all his body filleth
With wanton lightsomeness in every part.

17

Naked he goeth, but with sprightly wings
Red, iridescent, are his shoulders fledged.
His weapons are a bow he deftly strings,
And little arrows barb'd and keenly edged;
And these he shooteth true; but else the youth
For all his seeming recketh naught of truth,
But most deceiveth where he most is pledged.

18

'Tis he that maketh in men's heart a strife
Between remorseful reason and desire,
Till with life lost they lose the love of life,
And by their own hands wretchedly expire;
Or slain in bloody rivalries they miss
Even the short embracement of their bliss,
His smile of fury and his kiss of fire.

19

He makes the strong man weak, the weak man wild;
Ruins great business and purpose high;
Brings down the wise to folly reconciled,
And martial captains on their knees to sigh:
He changeth dynasties, and on the head
Of duteous heroes, who for honour bled,
Smircheth the laurel that can never die.

20

Him then she call'd, and gravely kissing told
The great dishonour to her godhead done;
And how, if he from that in heaven would hold,

On earth he must maintain it as her son;
The rather that his weapons were most fit,
As was his skill ordain'd to champion it;
And flattering thus his ready zeal she won.

21

Whereon she quickly led him down on earth,
And show'd him PSYCHE, thus the maid was named;
Whom when she show'd, but could not hide her
    worth,
She grew with envy tenfold more enflamed.
"But if," she cried, "thou smite her as I bid,
Soon shall our glory of this affront be rid,
And she and all her likes for ever shamed.

22

"Make her to love the loathliest, basest wretch,
Deform'd in body, and of moonstruck mind,
A hideous brute and vicious, born to fetch
Anger from dogs and cursing from the blind.
And let her passion for the monster be
As shameless and detestable as he
Is most extreme and vile of humankind."

23

Which said, when he agreed, she spake no more,
But left him to his task, and took her way
Beside the ripples of the shell-strewn shore,
The southward stretching margin of a bay,
Whose sandy curves she pass'd, and taking stand
Upon its taper horn of furthest land,
Lookt left and right to rise and set of day.

24

Fair was the sight; for now though full an hour
The sun had sunk she saw the evening light
In shifting colour to the zenith tower,
And grow more gorgeous ever and more bright.
Bathed in the warm and comfortable glow,
The fair delighted queen forgot her woe,
And watch'd the unwonted pageant of the night.

25

Broad and low down, where late the sun had been,
A wealth of orange-gold was thickly shed,
Fading above into a field of green,

Like apples ere they ripen into red;
Then to the height a variable hue
Of rose and pink and crimson freak'd with blue,
And olive-border'd clouds o'er lilac led.

26

High in the opposèd west the wondering moon
All silvery green in flying green was fleec't;
And round the blazing South the splendour soon
Caught all the heaven, and ran to North and East;
And Aphrodite knew the thing was wrought
By cunning of Poseidon, and she thought
She would go see with whom he kept his feast.

27

Swift to her wish came swimming on the waves
His lovely ocean nymphs, her guides to be,
The Nereids all, who live among the caves
And valleys of the deep, Cymodocè,
Agavè, blue-eyed Hallia and Nesæa,
Speio, and Thoë, Glaucè and Actæa,
Iaira, Melitè and Amphinomè,

28

Apseudès and Nemertès, Callianassa,
Cymothoë, Thaleia, Limnorrhea,
Clymenè, Ianeira and Ianassa,
Doris and Panopè and Galatea,
Dynamenè, Dexamenè and Maira,
Ferusa, Doto, Proto, Callianeira,
Amphithoë, Oreithuia and Amathea.

29

And after them sad Melicertes drave
His chariot, that with swift unfellied wheel,
By his two dolphins drawn along the wave,
Flew as they plunged, yet did not dip nor reel,
But like a plough that shears the heavy land
Stood on the flood, and back on either hand
O'erturn'd the briny furrow with its keel.

30

Behind came Tritons, that their conches blew,
Greenbearded, tail'd like fish, all sleek and stark ;
And hippocampi tamed, a bristly crew,

The browzers of old Proteus' weedy park,
Whose chiefer Mermen brought a shell for boat,
And balancing its hollow fan afloat,
Push'd it to shore and bade the queen embark:

31

And then the goddess stept upon the shell
Which took her weight; and others threw a train
Of soft silk o'er her, that unfurl'd to swell
In sails, at breath of flying Zephyrs twain;
And all her way with foam in laughter strewn,
With stir of music and of conches blown,
Was Aphrodite launch'd upon the main.

APRIL

1

BUT fairest Psyche still in favour rose,
  Nor knew the jealous power against her sworn;
And more her beauty now surpass't her foe's,
Since 'twas transfigured by the spirit forlorn,
That writeth, to the perfecting of grace,
Immortal question in a mortal face,
The vague desire whereunto man is born.

2

Already in good time her sisters both,
Whose honest charms were never famed as hers,
With princes of the isle had plighted troth,
And gone to rule their foreign courtiers;
But she, exalted evermore beyond
Their loveliness, made yet no lover fond,
And gain'd but number to her worshippers.

3

To joy in others' joy had been her lot,
And now that that was gone she wept to see
How her transcendent beauty overshot
The common aim of all felicity.
For love she sigh'd; and had some peasant rude
For true love's sake in simple passion woo'd,
Then Psyche had not scorn'd his wife to be.

4

For what is Beauty, if it doth not fire
The loving answer of an eager soul?
Since 'tis the native food of man's desire,
And doth to good our varying world control;
Which, when it was not, was for Beauty's sake
Desired and made by Love, who still doth make
A beauteous path thereon to Beauty's goal.

5

Should all men by some hateful venom die,
The pity were that o'er the unpeopl'd sphere
The sun would still bedeck the evening sky

c

And the unimaginable hues appear,
With none to mark the rose and gold and green;
That Spring should walk the earth, and nothing seen
Of her fresh delicacy year by year.

6

And if some beauteous things,—whose heavenly worth
And function overpass our mortal sense,—
Lie waste and unregarded on the earth
By reason of our gross intelligence,
These are not vain, because in nature's scheme
It lives that we shall grow from dream to dream
In time to gather an enchantment thence.

7

Even as we see the fairest works of men
Awhile neglected, and the makers die;
But Truth comes weeping to their graves, and then
Their fames victoriously mounting high
Do battle with the regnant names of eld,
To win their seats; as when the Gods rebel'd
Against their sires and drave them from the sky.

8

But to be praised for beauty and denied
The meed of beauty, this was yet unknown :
The best and bravest men have ever vied
To win the fairest women for their own.
  Thus Psyche spake, or reason'd in her mind,
Disconsolate, and with self-pity pined,
In the deserted halls wandering alone.

9

And grievèd grew the King to see her woe :
And blaming first the gods for her disease,
He purposed to their oracle to go
To question how he might their wrath appease,
Or, if that might not be, the worst to hear,—
Which is the last poor hope of them that fear.—
  So he took ship upon the northern seas,

10

And journeying to the shrine of Delphi went,
The temple of Apollo Pythian,
Where when the god he question'd if 'twas meant

That Psyche should be wed, and to what man,
The tripod shook, and o'er the vaporous well
The chanting Pythoness gave oracle,
And thus in priestly verse the sentence ran:

11

High on the topmost rock with funeral feast
Convey and leave the maid nor look to find
A mortal husband, but a savage beast,
The viperous scourge of gods and humankind;
Who shames and vexes all, and as he flies
With sword and fire, Zeus trembles in the skies,
And groans arise from souls to hell consign'd.

12

With which reply the King return'd full sad:
For though he nothing more might understand,
Yet in the bitter bidding that he had
No man made question of the plain command,
That he must sacrifice the tender flower
Of his own blood to a demonian power,
Upon the rocky mount with his own hand.

13

Some said that she to Talos was devote,
The metal giant, who with mile-long stride
Cover'd the isle, walking around by rote
Thrice every day at his appointed tide;
Who shepherded the sea-goats on the coast,
And, as he past, caught up and live would roast,
Pressing them to his burning ribs and side:

14

Whose head was made of fine gold-beaten work,
Of silver pure his arms and gleaming chest,
Thence of green-bloomèd bronze far as the fork,
Of iron weather-rusted all the rest.
One single vein he had, which running down
From head to foot was open in his crown,
And closèd by a nail; such was this pest.

15

A little while they spent in sad delay,
Then order'd, as the oracle had said,
The cold feast and funereal display

Wherewith the fated bridal should be sped:
And their black pageantry and vain despairing
When Psyche saw, and for herself preparing
The hopeless ceremonial of the dead,

16

Then spake she to the King and said "O Sire,
Why wilt thou veil those venerable eyes
With piteous tears, which must of me require
More tears again than for myself arise?
Then, on the day my beauty first o'erstept
Its mortal place it had been well to have wept;
But now the fault beyond our ruing lies.

17

"As to be worship'd was my whole undoing,
So my submission must the forfeit pay:
And welcome were the morning of my wooing,
Tho' after it should dawn no other day.
Up to the mountain! for I hear the voice
Of my belovèd on the winds, *Rejoice,
Arise, my love, my fair one, and come away!*"

18

With such distemper'd speech, that little cheer'd
Her mourning house, she went to choose with care
The raiment for her day of wedlock weird,
Her body as for burial to prepare ;
But laved with bridal water, from the stream
Where Hera bathed ; for still her fate supreme
Was doubtful, whether Love or Death it were :

19

Love that is made of joy, and Death of fear :
Nay, but not these held Psyche in suspense ;
Hers was the hope that following by the bier
Boweth its head beneath the dark⸝immense :
Her fear the dread of life that turns to hide
Its tragic tears, what hour the happy bride
Ventures for love her maiden innocence.

20

They set on high upon the bridal wain
Her bed for bier, and yet no corpse thereon ;
But like as when unto a warrior slain

And not brought home the ceremonies done
Are empty, for afar his body brave
Lies lost, deep buried by the wandering wave,
Or 'neath the foes his fury fell upon,

21

So was her hearse: and with it went afore,
Singing the solemn dirge that moves to tears,
The singers; and behind, clad as for war,
The King uncrown'd among his mournful peers,
All 'neath their armour robed in linen white;
And in their left were shields, and in their right
Torches they bore aloft instead of spears.

22

And next the virgin tribe in white forth sail'd,
With wreaths of dittany; and 'midst them there
Went Psyche, all in lily-whiteness veil'd,
The white Quince-blossom chapleting her hair:
And last the common folk, a weeping crowd,
Far as the city-gates with wailings loud
Follow'd the sad procession in despair.

23

Thus forth and up the mount they went, until
The funeral chariot must be left behind,
Since road was none for steepness of the hill;
And slowly by the narrow path they wind:
All afternoon their white and scatter'd file
Toil'd on distinct, ascending many a mile
Over the long brown slopes and crags unkind.

24

But ere unto the snowy peak they came
Of that stormshapen pyramid so high,
'Twas evening, and with footsteps slow and lame
They gather'd up their lagging company:
And then her sire, even as Apollo bade,
Set on the topmost rock the hapless maid,
With trembling hands and melancholy cry.

25

And now the sun was sunk; only the peak
Flash'd like a jewel in the deepening blue:
And from the shade beneath none dared to speak,

But all look'd up, where glorified anew
Psyche sat islanded in living day.
Breathless they watcht her, till the last red ray
Fled from her lifted arm that waved adieu.

26

There left they her, turning with sad farewells
To haste their homeward course, as best they might:
But night was crowding up the barren fells,
And hid full soon their rocky path from sight;
And each unto his stumbling foot to hold
His torch was fain, for o'er the moon was roll'd
A mighty cloud from heaven, to blot her light.

27

And thro' the darkness for long while was seen
That armour'd train with waving fires to thread
Downwards, by pass, defile, and black ravine,
Each leading on the way that he was led.
Slowly they gain'd the plain, and one by one
Into the shadows of the woods were gone,
Or in the clinging mists were quench'd and fled.

28

But unto Psyche, pondering o'er her doom
In tearful silence on her stony chair,
A Zephyr straying out of heaven's wide room
Rush'd down, and gathering round her unaware
Fill'd with his breath her vesture and her veil,
And like a ship, that crowding all her sail
Leans to accompany the tranquil air,

29

She yielded, and was borne with swimming brain
And airy joy, along the mountain side,
Till, hid from earth by ridging summits twain,
They came upon a valley deep and wide;
Where the strong Zephyr with his burden sank,
And laid her down upon a grassy bank,
'Mong thyme and violets and daisies pied.

30

And straight upon the touch of that sweet bed
Both woe and wonder melted fast away:
And sleep with gentle stress her sense o'erspread,

Gathering as darkness doth on drooping day:
And nestling to the ground, she slowly drew
Her wearied limbs together, and, ere she knew,
Wrapt in forgetfulness and slumber lay.

MAY

1

AFTER long sleep when Psyche first awoke
Among the grasses 'neath the open skies,
And heard the mounting larks, whose carol spoke
Delighted invitation to arise,
She lay as one who after many a league
Hath slept off memory with his long fatigue,
And waking knows not in what place he lies:

2

Anon her quickening thought took up its task,
And all came back as it had happ'd o'ernight;
The sad procession of the wedding mask,
The melancholy toiling up the height,
The solitary rock where she was left;
And thence in dark and airy waftage reft,
How on the flowers she had been disburden'd light.

3

Thereafter she would rise and see what place
That voyage had its haven in, and found
She stood upon a little hill, whose base
Shelved off into the valley all around;
And all round that the steep cliffs rose away,
Save on one side where to the break of day
The widening dale withdrew in falling ground.

4.

There, out from over sea, and scarce so high
As she, the sun above his watery blaze
Upbroke the grey dome of the morning sky,
And struck the island with his level rays;
Sifting his gold thro' lazy mists, that still
Climb'd on the shadowy roots of every hill,
And in the tree-tops breathed their silvery haze.

5

At hand on either side there was a wood;
And on the upward lawn, that sloped between,
Not many paces back a temple stood,

By even steps ascending from the green;
With shaft and pediment of marble made,
It fill'd the passage of the rising glade,
And there withstay'd the sun in dazzling sheen.

6

Too fair for human art, so Psyche thought,
It might the fancy of some god rejoice;
Like to those halls which lame Hephæstos wrought,
Original, for each god to his choice,
In high Olympus; where his matchless lyre
Apollo wakes, and the responsive choir
Of Muses sing alternate with sweet voice.

7

Wondering she drew anigh, and in a while
Went up the steps as she would entrance win,
And faced her shadow 'neath the peristyle
Upon the golden gate, whose flanges twin—
As there she stood, irresolute at heart
To try—swung to her of themselves apart;
Whereat she past between and stood within.

8

A foursquare court it was with marble floor'd,
Embay'd about with pillar'd porticoes,
That echo'd in a somnolent accord
The music of a fountain, which arose
Sparkling in air, and splashing in its tank;
Whose wanton babble, as it swell'd or sank,
Gave idle voice to silence and repose.

9

Thro' doors beneath the further colonnade,
Like a deep cup's reflected glooms of gold,
The inner rooms glow'd with inviting shade:
And, standing in the court, she might behold
Cedar, and silk, and silver; and that all
The pargeting of ceiling and of wall
Was fresco'd o'er with figures manifold.

10

Then making bold to go within, she heard
Murmur of gentle welcome in her ear;
And seeing none that coud have spoken word,

She waited : when again **Lady, draw near ;**
Enter ! was cried; and now more voices came
From all the air around calling her name,
And bidding her rejoice and have no fear.

11

And one, if she would rest, would show her bed,
Pillow'd for sleep, with fragrant linen fine ;
One, were she hungry, had a table spread
Like as the high gods have it when they dine :
Or, would she bathe, were those would heat the bath;
The joyous cries contending in her path,
Psyche, they said, **What wilt thou? all is thine.**

12

Then Psyche would have thank'd their service true,
But that she fear'd her echoing words might scare
Those sightless tongues; and well by dream she knew
The voices of the messengers of prayer,
Which fly upon the gods' commandment, when
They answer the supreme desires of men,
Or for a while in pity hush their care.

D

13

'Twas fancy's consummation, and because
She would do joy no curious despite,
She made no wonder how the wonder was;
Only concern'd to take her full delight.
So to the bath,—what luxury coud be
Better enhanced by eyeless ministry?—
She follows with the voices that invite.

14

There being deliciously refresht, from soil
Of earth made pure by water, fire, and air,
They clad her in soft robes of Asian toil,
Scented, that in her queenly wardrobe were;
And led her forth to dine, and all around
Sang as they served, the while a choral sound
Of strings unseen and reeds the burden bare.

15

P athetic strains and passionate they wove,
U rgent in ecstasies of heavenly sense;
R esponsive rivalries, that, while they strove,

C ombined in full harmonious suspense,
E ntrancing wild desire, then fell at last
L ull'd in soft closes, and with gay contrast
L aunch'd forth their fresh unwearied excellence.

16

Now Psyche, when her twofold feast was o'er,
Would feed her eye; and choosing for her guide
A low-voiced singer, bade her come explore
The wondrous house; until on every side
As surfeited with beauty, and seeing nought
But what was rich and fair beyond her thought,
And all her own, thus to the voice she cried:

17

"Am I indeed a goddess, or is this
But to be dead; and through the gates of death
Passing unwittingly doth man not miss
Body nor memory nor living breath;
Nor by demerits of his deeds is cast,
But, paid with the desire he holdeth fast,
Is holp with all his heart imagineth?"

18

But her for all reply the wandering tongue
Call'd to the chamber where her bed was laid,
With flower'd broideries of linen hung:
And round the walls in painting were portray'd
Love's victories over the gods renown'd.
Ares and Aphrodite here lay bound
In the fine net that dark Hephæstus made:

19

Here Zeus, in likeness of a tawny bull,
Stoop'd on the Cretan shore his mighty knee,
While off his back Europa beautiful
Stept pale against the blue Carpathian sea;
And here Apollo, as he caught amazed
Daphne, for lo! her hands shot forth upraised
In leaves, her feet were rooted like a tree:

20

Here Dionysos, springing from his car
At sight of Ariadne; here uplept
Adonis to the chase, breaking the bar

Of Aphrodite's arm for love who wept:
He spear in hand, with leashèd dogs at strain;
A marvellous work.   But Psyche soon grown fain
Of rest, betook her to her bed and slept.

21

Nor long had slept, when at a sudden stir
She woke; and one, that thro' the dark made way,
Drew near, and stood beside; and over her
The curtain rustl'd.   Trembling now she lay,
Fainting with terror: till upon her face
A kiss, and with two gentle arms' embrace,
A voice that call'd her name in loving play.

22

Though for the darkness she coud nothing see,
She wish'd not then for what the night denied:
This was the lover she had lack'd, and she,
Loving his loving, was his willing bride.
O'erjoy'd she slept again, o'erjoy'd awoke
At break of morn upon her love to look;
When lo! his empty place lay by her side.

23

So all that day she spent in company
Of the soft voices; and Of right, they said,
Art thou our Lady now. Be happily
The bridal morrow by thy servants sped.
But she but long'd for night, if that might bring
Her lover back; and he on secret wing
Came with the dark, and in the darkness fled.

24

And this was all her life; for every night
He came, and though his name she never learn'd,
Nor was his image yielded to her sight
At morn or eve, she neither look'd nor yearn'd
Beyond the joy she had: and custom brought
An ease to pleasure; nor would Psyche's thought
Have ever to her earthly home return'd,

25

But that one night he said "Psyche, my soul,
Sad danger threatens us: thy sisters twain
Come to the mountain top, whence I thee stole,

And thou wilt hear their voices thence complain.
Answer them not : for it must end our love
If they should hear or spy thee from above."
And Psyche said " Their cry shall be in vain."

26

But being again alone, she thought 'twas hard
On her own blood ;' and blamed her joy as thief
Of theirs, her comfort which their comfort barr'd ;
When she their care might be their care's relief.
All day she brooded on her father's woe,
And when at night her lover kisst her, lo !
Her tender face was wet with tears of grief.

27

Then question'd why she wept, she all confest ;
And begg'd of him she might but once go nigh
To set her sire's and sisters' fears at rest ;
Till he for pity coud not but comply :
"Only if they should ask thee of thy love
Discover nothing to their ears above."
And Psyche said " In vain shall be their cry."

28

And yet with day no sooner was alone,
Than she for loneliness her promise rued:
That having so much pleasure for her own,
'Twas all unshared and spent in solitude.
And when at night her love flew to his place,
More than afore she shamed his fond embrace,
And piteously with tears her plaint renew'd.

29

The more he now denied, the more she wept;
Nor would in anywise be comforted,
Unless her sisters, on the Zephyr swept,
Should in those halls be one day bathed and fed,
And see themselves the palace where she reign'd.
And he by force of tears at last constrain'd,
Granted her wish unwillingly, and said:

30

" Much to our peril hast thou won thy will;
Thy sisters' love, seeing thee honour'd so,
Will sour to envy, and with jealous skill

Will pry to learn the thing thou must not know.
Answer not, nor inquire; for know that I
The day thou seest my face far hence shall fly,
And thou anew to bitterest fate must go."

31

But Psyche said "Thy love is more than life;
To have thee leaveth nothing to be won :
For should the noonday prove me to be wife
Even of the beauteous Eros, who is son ·
Of Cypris, I could never love thee more."
Whereat he fondly kisst her o'er and o'er,
And peace was 'twixt them till the night was done.

SECOND QUARTER

Summer

*Psyche's sisters, snaring her to destruction, are
themselves destroyed.*

JUNE

1

A ND truly need there was to the old King
For consolation: since the mournful day
Of Psyche's fate he took no comforting,
But only for a speedy death would pray;
And on his head his hair grew silver-white.
—Such on life's topmost bough is sorrow's blight,
When the stout heart is cankering to decay.

2

Which when his daughters learnt, they both were
quick
Comfort and solace to their sire to lend.
But as not seldom they who nurse the sick
Will take the malady from them they tend,
So happ'd it now; for they who fail'd to cheer
Grew sad themselves, and in that palace drear
Increased the evil that they came to mend.

3

And them the unhappy father sent to seek
Where Psyche had been left, if they might find
What monster held her on the savage peak;
Or if she there had died of hunger pined,
And, by wild eagles stript, her scatter'd bones
Might still be gather'd from the barren stones;
Or if her fate had left no trace behind.

4

So just upon this time her sisters both
Climb'd on the cliff that hung o'er Psyche's vale;
And finding there no sign, to leave were loth
Ere well assured she lurk'd not within hail.
So calling loud her name, "Psyche!" they cried,
"Psyche, O Psyche!" and when none replied
They sank upon the rocks to weep and wail.

5

But Psyche heard their voices where she sat,
And summoning the Zephyr bade him fleet
Those mourners down unto the grassy plat

'Midst of her garden, where she had her seat,
Then from the dizzy steep the wondering pair
Came swiftly sinking on his buoyant air,
And stood upon the terrace at her feet.

6

Upsprang she then, and kiss'd them and embraced,
And said "Lo, here am I, I whom ye mourn.
I am not dead, nor tortured, nor disgraced,
But blest above all days since I was born :
Wherefore be glad. Enter my home and see
How little cause has been to grieve for me,
And my desertion on the rocks forlorn."

7

So entering by the golden gate, or e'er
The marvel of their hither flight had waned,
Fresh wonder took them now, for everywhere
Their eyes that lit on beauty were enchain'd;
And Psyche's airy service, as she bade,
Perform'd its magic office, and display'd
The riches of the palace where she reign'd.

8

And through the perfumed chambers they were led,
And bathed therein; and after, set to sup,
Were upon dreamlike delicacies fed,
And wine more precious than its golden cup.
Till seeing nothing lack'd and naught was theirs,
Their happiness fell from them unawares,
And bitter envy in their hearts sprang up.

9

At last one said "Psyche, since not alone
Thou livest here in joy, as well we wot,
Who is the man who should these wonders own,
Or god, I say, and still appeareth not?
What is his name? What rank and guise hath he,
Whom winds and spirits serve, who honoureth thee
Above all others in thy blissful lot?"

10

But Psyche when that wistful speech she heard
Was ware of all her spouse had warn'd her of:
And uttering a disingenuous word,

Said "A youth yet unbearded is my love;
He goeth hunting on the plains to-day,
And with his dogs hath wander'd far away;
And not till eve can he return above."

11

Then fearing to be nearer plied, she rose
And brought her richest jewels one by one,
Bidding them choose and take whate'er they chose;
And beckoning the Zephyr spake anon
That he should waft her sisters to the peak;
The which he did, and, ere they more coud speak,
They rose on high, and in the wind were gone.

12

Nor till again they came upon the road,
Which from the mountain shoulder o'er the plain
Led to the city of their sire's abode,
Found they their tongues, though full of high disdain
Their hearts were, but kept silence, till the strength
Of pride and envious hatred burst at length
In voice, and thus the elder gan complain:

E

13

"Cruel and unjust fortune! that of three
Sisters, whose being from one fountain well'd,
Exalts the last so high from her degree,
And leaves the first to be so far excel'd.
My husband is a poor and niggard churl
To him, whoe'er he be, that loves the girl.
Oh! in what godlike state her house is held!"

14

"Ay," said the other, "to a gouty loon
Am I not wedded? Lo! thy hurt is mine:
But never call me woman more, if soon
I cannot lure her from her height divine.
Nay, she shall need her cunning wit to save
The wealth of which so grudgingly she gave;
Wherefore thy hand and heart with me combine.

15

"She but received us out of pride, to show
Her state, well deeming that her happiness
Was little worth while there was none to know;

So is our lot uninjured if none guess.
Reveal we nothing therefore, but the while
Together scheme this wanton to beguile,
And bring her boasting godhead to distress."

16

So fresh disordering their dress and hair,
With loud lament they to their sire return,
Telling they found not Psyche anywhere,
And of her sure mischance could nothing learn :
And with that lie the wounded man they slew,
Hiding the saving truth which well they knew;
Nor did his piteous grief their heart concern.

17

Meanwhile her unknown lover did not cease
To warn poor Psyche how her sisters plan'd
To undermine her love and joy and peace;
And urged how well she might their wiles withstand,
By keeping them from her delight aloof :
For better is security than proof,
And malice held afar than near at hand.

18

"And, dearest wife," he said, "since 'tis not long
Ere one will come to share thy secrecy,
And be thy babe and mine; let nothing wrong
The happy months of thy maternity.
If thou keep trust, then shalt thou see thy child
A god; but if to pry thou be beguiled,
The lot of both is death and misery."

19

Then Psyche's simple heart was fill'd with joy,
And counting to herself the months and days,
Look'd for the time, when she should bear a boy
To be her growing stay and godlike praise.
And "O be sure," she said, "be sure, my pride
Having so rich a promise cannot slide,
Even if my love coud fail which thee obeys."

20

And so most happily her life went by,
In thoughts of love dear to her new estate;
Until at length the evil day drew nigh,

When now her sisters, joined in jealous hate,
Set forth again, and plotted by the way
How they might best allure her to betray
Her secret; with what lie their angle bait.

21

That night her husband spake to her, and said
 — "Psyche, thy sisters come : and when they climb
The peak they will not tarry to be sped
Down by the Zephyr, as that other time,
But winging to the wind will cast themselves
Out in the air, and on the rocky shelves
Be dasht, and pay the penalty of crime.

22

"So let it be, and so shall we be saved."
Which meditated vengeance of his fear
When Psyche heard, now for their life she craved,
Whose mere distress erewhile had toucht her near.
Around her lover's neck her arms she threw,
And pleaded for them by her faith so true,
Although they went on doom in judgment clear.

23

In terror of bloodguiltiness she now
Forgot all other danger; she adjured;
Or using playfulness deep sobs would plow
Her soft entreaties, not to be endured:
Till he at last was fain once more to grant
The service of the Zephyr, to enchant
That wicked couple from their fate assured.

24

So ere 'twas noon were noises at the door
Of knocking loud and voices high in glee;
Such as within that vale never before
Had been, and now seem'd most unmeet to be.
And Psyche blush'd, though being alone, and rose
To meet her sisters and herself unclose
The gate that made them of her palace free.

25

Fondly she kiss'd them, and with kindly cheer
Sought to amuse; and they with outward smile
O'ermask'd their hate, and called her sweet and dear,

Finding affection easy to beguile:
And all was smooth, until at last one said
"Tell us, I pray, to whom 'tis thou art wed;
'Mong gods or men, what is his rank and style?

26

"Thou canst not think to hide the truth from us,
Who knew thy peevish sorrows when a maid,
And see thee now so glad and rapturous,
As changed from what thou wert as light from shade;
Thy jewels, too, the palace of a king,
Nor least the serviceable spiriting,
By everything thy secret is betray'd:

27

"And yet thou talkest of thy wondrous man
No more than if his face thou didst not know."
At which incontinently she began,
Forgetful of her word a month ago,
Answering "A merchant rich, of middle age,
My husband is; and o'er his features sage
His temples are already touch'd with snow.

28

"But 'gainst his wish since hither ye were brought
'Twere best depart."   Then her accustom'd spell
Sped them upon the summit quick as thought;
And being alone her doing pleased her well:
So was she vext to find her love at night
More sad than ever, of her sisters' spite
Speaking as one that coud the end foretell.

29

"And ere long," said he, "they will spy again:
Let them be dash'd upon the rocks and die;
'Tis they must come to death or thou to pain,
To separation, Psyche, thou and I;
Nay, and our babe to ill.   I therefore crave
Thou wilt not even once more these vipers save,
Nor to thy love his only boon deny."

30

But Psyche would not think her sisters' crime
So gross and strange, nor coud her danger see;
Since 'twere so easy, if at any time

They show'd the venom of their hearts, that she
Should fan them off upon the willing gust.
So she refused, and claiming truer trust,
Would in no wise unto their death agree.

JULY

1

" WHAT think you, sister : " thus one envious
   fiend
To other spake upon their homeward route,
" What of the story that our wit hath glean'd
Of this mysterious lover, who can shoot
In thirty days from beardless youth to prime,
With wisdom in his face before his time,
And snowy locks upon his head to boot ? "

2

" Ay," said the other, " true, she lied not well ;
And thence I gather knows no more than we :
For surely 'tis a spirit insensible
To whom she is wedded, one she cannot see.
'Tis that I fear ; for if 'tis so, her child
Will be a god, and she a goddess styled,
Which, though I die to let it, shall not be.

3

"Lament we thus no longer.   Come, consult
What may be done."   And home they came at night,
Yet not to rest, but of their plots occult
Sat whispering on their beds; and ere 'twas light
Resolving on the deed coud not defer;
But roused the sleeping house with sudden stir,
And sallied forth alone to work their spite.

4

And with the noon were climb'd upon the peak,
And swam down on the Zephyr as before;
But now with piercing cry and doleful shriek
They force their entrance through the golden door.
Feigning the urgency of bitter truth;
Such as deforms a friendly face with ruth,
When kindness may not hide ill tidings more.

5

Then Psyche when she heard their wailful din,
And saw their countenances wan and worn
With travel, vigil, and disfiguring sin,

Their hair dishevel'd and their habits torn,
For trembling scarce could ask what ill had hapt;
And they alert with joy to see her trapt,
Launch'd forth amain, and on their drift were borne.

6

"O Psyche, happiest certainly and blest
Up to this hour," they said, "thou surely wert,
Being of thy fearful peril unpossest;
Which now we would not tell but to avert.
But we in solemn truth thy spouse have found
To be the dragon of this mountain ground,
Who holds thee here to work thy shame and hurt.

7

"As yesternight we rode upon the wind
He issued to pursue us from the wood;
We saw his back, that through the tree-tops finn'd,
His fiery eyes glared from their wrinkl'd hood.
Lo, now betimes the oracle, which said
How to the savage beast thou shouldst be wed,
Is plainly for thy safety understood.

8

"Long time hath he been known to all that dwell
Upon the plain; but now his secret lair
Have we discover'd, which none else coud tell:
Though many women fallen in his snare
Hath he enchanted; who, tradition saith,
Taste love awhile, ere to their cruel death
They pass in turn upon the summits bare.

9

"Fly with us while thou mayst: no more delay;
Renounce the spells of this accursed vale.
We come to save thee, but we dare not stay;
Among these sightless spirits our senses quail.
Fly with us, fly!"   Then Psyche, for her soul
Was soft and simple, lost her self-control,
And, thinking only of the horrid tale,

10

"Dear sisters," said she, and her sobbing speech
Was broken by her terror, "it is true
That much hath hapt to stablish what ye teach;

For ne'er hath it been granted me to view
My husband; and, for aught I know, he may
Be even that cruel dragon, which ye say
Peer'd at you from the forest to pursue.

11

"'Tis sure that scarcely can I win his grace
To see you here; and still he mischief vows
If ever I should ask to see his face,
Which, coming in the dark, he ne'er allows.
Therefore, if ye can help, of pity show,
Since doubt I must, how I may come to know
What kind of spirit it is that is my spouse."

12

Then to her cue the younger was afore:
" Hide thou a razor," cried she, " near thy bed;
And have a lamp prepared, but whelm thereo'er
Some cover, that no light be from it shed.
And when securely in first sleep he lies,
Look on him well, and ere he can arise,
Gashing his throat, cut off his hideous head."

13

Which both persuading, off they flew content,
Divining that whate'er she was forbid
Was by her lover for her safety meant,
Which only coud be sure while he was hid.
  But Psyche, to that miserable deed
Being now already in her mind agreed,
Wander'd alone, and knew not what she did.

14

Now she would trust her lover, now in turn
Made question of his bidding as unjust;
But thirsting curiosity to learn
His secret overcame her simple trust,
O'ercame her spoken troth, o'ercame her fear;
And she prepared, as now the hour drew near,
The mean contrivances, nor felt disgust.

15

She set the lamp beneath a chair, and cloked
Thickly its rebel lustre from the eye:
And laid the knife, to mortal keenness stroked,

Within her reach, where she was wont to lie:
And took her place full early; but her heart
Beat fast, and stay'd her breath with sudden start,
Feeling her lover's arm laid fond thereby.

16

But when at last he slept, then she arose,
All faint and tremulous: and though it be
That wrong betrayeth innocence with shews
Of novelty, its guilt from shame to free,
Yet 'twas for shame her hand so strangely shook
That held the steel, and from the cloke that took
The lamp, and raised it o'er the bed to see.

17

She had some fear she might not well discern
By that small flame a monster in the gloom;
When lo! the air about her seem'd to burn,
And bright celestial radiance fill'd the room.
Too plainly O she saw, O fair to see!
Eros, 'twas Eros' self, her lover, he,
The God of love, reveal'd in deathless bloom.

18

Her fainting strength forsook her; on her knees
Down by the bed she sank; the shameless knife
Fell flashing, and her heart took thought to seize
Its desperate haft, and end her wicked life.
Yet coud she not her loving eyes withdraw
From her fair sleeping lover, whom she saw
Only to know she was no more his wife.

19

O treasure of all treasures, late her own!
O loss above all losses, lost for aye!
Since there was no repentance coud atone
For her dishonour, nor her fate withstay.
But yet 'twas joy to have her love in sight;
And, to the rapture yielding while she might,
She gazed upon his body where he lay.

20

Above all mortal beauty, as was hers,
She saw a rival; but if passion's heart
Be rightly read by subtle questioners,

F

It owns a wanton and a gentler part.
And Psyche wonder'd, noting every sign
By which the immortal God, her spouse divine,
Betray'd the image of our earthly art;

21

His thickly curling hair, his ruddy cheeks,
And pouting lips, his soft and dimpl'd chin,
The full and cushion'd eye, that idly speaks
Of self-content and vanity within,
The forward, froward ear, and smooth to touch
His body sleek, but rounded overmuch
For dignity of mind and pride akin.

22

She noted that the small irradiant wings,
That from his shoulders lay along at rest,
Were yet disturb'd with airy quiverings,
As if some wakeful spirit his blood possest;
She feared he was awaking, but they kept
Their sweet commotion still, and still he slept,
And still she gazed with never-tiring zest.

23

And now the colour of her pride and joy
Outflush'd the hue of Eros; she, so cold,
To have fired the passion of the heartless boy,
Whom none in heaven or earth were found to hold!
Psyche, the earthborn, to be prized above
The heavenly Graces by the God of love,
And worshipt by his wantonness untold!

24

Nay, for that very thing she loved him more,
More than herself her sweet self's complement:
Until the sight of him again upbore
Her courage, and renew'd her vigour spent.
And looking now around, she first espied
Where at the bed's foot, cast in haste aside,
Lay his full quiver, and his bow unbent.

25

One of those darts, of which she had heard so oft,
She took to try if 'twas so very keen;
And held its point against her finger soft

So gently, that to touch it scarce was seen;
Yet was she sharply prickt, and felt the fire
Run through her veins; and now a strange desire
Troubl'd her heart, which ne'er before had been:

26

Straight sprang she to her lover on the bed,
And kisst his cheek, and was not satisfied:
When, O the lamp, held ill-balanced o'erhead,
One drop of burning oil spill'd from its side
On Eros' naked shoulder as he slept,
Who wakened by the sudden smart uplept
Upon the floor, and all the mischief eyed.

27

With nervous speed he seized his bow, and past
Out of the guilty chamber at a bound;
But Psyche, following his flight as fast,
Caught him, and crying threw her arms around:
Till coming to the court he rose in air;
And she, close clinging in her last despair,
Was dragg'd, and then lost hold and fell to ground.

28

Wailing she fell; but he, upon the roof
Staying his feet, awhile his flight delay'd:
And turning to her as he stood aloof
Beside a cypress, whose profoundest shade
Drank the reflections of the dreamy night
In its stiff pinnacle, the nimble light
Of million stars upon his body play'd:

29

"O simple-hearted Psyche," thus he spake,
And she upraised her piteous eyes and hands,
"O simple-hearted Psyche, for thy sake
I dared to break my mother's stern commands;
And gave thee godlike marriage in the place
Of vilest shame; and, not to hurt thy grace,
Spared thee my arrows, which no heart withstands.

30

" But thou, for doubt I was some evil beast,
Hast mock'd the warning of my love, to spy
Upon my secret, which concern'd thee least,

Seeing that thy joy was never touch'd thereby.
By faithless prying thou hast work'd thy fall,
And, even as I foretold thee, losest all
For looking on thy happiness too nigh.

31

"Which loss may be thine ample punishment.
But to those fiends, by whom thou wert misled,
Go tell each one in turn that I have sent
This message, that I love her in thy stead;
And bid them by their love haste hither soon."
Whereat he fled; and Psyche in a swoon
Fell back upon the marble floor as dead.

AUGUST

1

WHEN from the lowest ebbing of her blood
　　The fluttering pulses thrill'd and swell'd
　again,
Her stricken heart recovering force to flood
With life the sunken conduits of her brain,
Then Psyche, where she had fallen, numb and cold
Arose, but scarce her quaking sense control'd,
Seeing the couch where she that night had lain.

2

The level sunbeams search'd the grassy ground
For diamond dewdrops.　Ah ! was this the place ?
Where was the court, her home ? she look'd around
And question'd with her memory for a space.
There was the cypress, there the well-known wood,
That wall'd the spot : 'twas here her palace stood,
As surely as 'twas vanish'd without trace.

3

Was all a dream? To think that all was dreamt
Were now the happier thought; but arguing o'er
That dream it was, she fell from her attempt,
Feeling the wifely burden that she bore.
Nay, true, 'twas true. She had had all and lost;
The joy, the reckless wrong, the heavy cost
Were hers, the dead end now, and woe in store.

4

What to be done? Fainting and shelterless
Upon the mountain it were death to bide:
And harbour knew she none, where her distress
Might comfort find, or love's dishonour hide;
Nor felt she any dread like that of home:
Yet forth she must, albeit to rove and roam
An outcast o'er the country far and wide.

5

Anon she marvel'd noting from the vale
A path lead downward to the plain below,
Crossing the very site, whereon the pale

Of all her joy had stood few hours ago ;
A run of mountain beasts, that keep their track
Through generations, and for ages back
Had trod the self-same footing to and fro.

6

That would she try : so forth she took her way,
Turning her face from the dishonour'd dell,
Adown the broadening eastward lawns, which lay
In gentle slant, till suddenly they fell
In sheer cliff ; whence the path that went around,
Clomb by the bluffs or e'er it downward wound
Beneath that precipice impassable.

7

There once she turn'd, and gazing up the slope
She bid the scene of all her joy adieu ;
" Ay, and farewell," she cried, " farewell to hope,
Since there is none will rescue me anew,
Who have kill'd God's perfection with a doubt."
Which said, she took the path that led about,
And hid the upland pleasance from her view.

8

But soon it left her, entering 'neath the shade
Of cedar old and russeted tall pine,
Whose mighty tops, seen from the thorny glade,
Belted the hills about; and now no sign
Had she to guide her, save the slow descent.
But swiftly o'er the springy floor she went,
And drew the odorous air like draughts of wine.

9

Then next she past a forest thick and dark
With heavy ilexes and platanes high,
And came to long lush grass; and now coud mark
By many a token that the plain was nigh.
When lo! a river: to whose brink at last
Being come, upon the bank her limbs she cast,
And through her sad tears watch'd the stream go by.

10

And now the thought came o'er her that in death
There was a cure for sorrow, that before
Her eyes ran Lethe, she might take one breath

Of water and be freed for evermore.
Leaning to look into her tomb, thereon
She saw the horror of her image wan,
And up she rose at height to leap from shore.

11

When suddenly a mighty voice, that fell
With fury on her ears, their sense to scare,
That bounding from the tree trunks like the yell
Of hundred brazen trumpets, cried " Forbear !
Forbear, fond maid, that froward step to take,
For life can cure the ills that love may make ;
But for the harm of death is no repair."

12

Then looking up she saw an uncouth form
Perch'd on the further bank, whose parted lips
Volley'd their friendly warning in a storm :
A man he might have been, but for the tips
Of horns appearing from his shaggy head,
For o'er his matted beard his face was red,
And all his shape was manlike to the hips.

13

In forehead low, keen eye, and nostril flat
He bore the human grace in mean degree,
But, set beneath his body squat and fat,
Legs like a goat's, and from the hairy knee
The shank fell spare ; and, though crosswise he put
His limbs in easeful posture, for the foot
The beast's divided hoof was plain to see.

14

Him then she knew the mighty choric God,
The great hill-haunting and tree-loving Pan ;
Whom Zeus had laught to see when first he trod
Olympus, neither god nor beast nor man :
Who every rocky peak and snowy crest
Of the Aspran mountains for his own possest,
And all their alps with bacchic rout o'erran.

15

Whom, when his pipe he plays on loud and sweet,
And o'er the fitted reeds his moist lip flees,
Around in measured step with nimble feet

Water-nymphs dance and Hamadryades :
And all the woodland's airy folk, who shun
Man's presence, to his frolic pastime run
From their perennial wells and sacred trees.

16

Now on his knee his pipe laid by, he spoke
With flippant tongue, wounding unwittingly
The heart he sought to cheer with jest and joke.
"And what hast thou to do with misery,"
He said, "who hast such beauty as might gain
The love of Eros ? Cast away thy pain,
And give thy soul to mirth and jollity.

17

"Thy mortal life is but a brittle vase,
But as thee list with wine or tears to fill ;
For all the drops therein are Ohs and Ahs
Of joy or grief according to thy will ;
And wouldst thou learn of me my merry way,
I'd teach thee change thy lover every day,
And prize the cup that thou wert fain to spill.

18

"Nay, if thou plunge thou shalt not drown nor sink,
For I will to thee o'er the stream afloat,
And bear thee safe; and O I know a drink
For care, that makes sweet music in the throat.
Come live with me, my love; I'll cure thy chance:
For I can laugh and quaff, and pipe and dance,
Swim like a fish, and caper like a goat."

19

Speaking, his brute divinity explored
The secret of her silence; and old Pan
Grew kind and told her of a shallow ford
Where lower down the stream o'er pebbles ran,
And one might pass at ease with ankles dry:
Whither she went, and crossing o'er thereby,
Her lonely wanderings through the isle began.

20

But none could tell, no, nor herself had told
Where food she found, or shelter through the land
By day or night; until by fate control'd

She came by steep ways to the southern strand,
Where, sacred to the Twins and Britomart,
Pent in its rocky theatre apart,
A little town stood on the level sand.

21

'Twas where her younger sister's husband reign'd:
And Psyche to the palace gate drew near,
Helplessly still by Eros' hest constrain'd,
And knocking begg'd to see her sister dear;
But when in state stepp'd down that haughty queen,
And saw the wan face spent with tears and teen,
She smiled, and said " Psyche, what dost thou here ? "

22

Then Psyche told how, having well employ'd
Their means, and done their bidding not amiss,
Looking on him her hand would have destroy'd,
'Twas Eros; whom in love leaning to kiss,
Even as she kisst, a drop of burning oil
Fall'n from the lamp had served her scheme to foil,
Discovering her in vision of her bliss;

23

Wherewith the god stung, like a startled bird
Arose in air, and she fell back in swoon;
"But ere he parted," said she, "he confer'd
On thee the irrecoverable boon
By prying lost to me: *Go tell*, he said,
Thy sister that I love her in thy stead,
And bid her by her love haste hither soon."

24

Which when that heart of malice heard, it took
The jealous fancy of her silly lust:
And pitilessly with triumphant look
She drank the flattery, and gave full trust;
And leaving Psyche ere she more could tell,
Ran off to bid her spouse for aye farewell,
And in his ear this ready lie she thrust:

25

"My dearest sister Psyche, she whose fate
We mourn'd, hath reappear'd alive and hale,
But brings sad news; my father dies: full late

These tidings come, but love may yet avail ;
Let me be gone." And stealing blind consent,
Forth on that well-remember'd road she went,
And climb'd upon the peak above the dale.

26

There on the topmost rock, where Psyche first
Had by her weeping sire been left to die,
She stood a moment, in her hope accurst
Being happy; and the cliffs took up her cry
With chuckling mockery from her tongue above,
Zephyr, sweet Zephyr, waft me to my love!
When off she lept upon his wings to fly.

27

But as a dead stone, from a height let fall,
Silent and straight is gather'd by the force
Of earth's vast mass upon its weight so small,
In speed increasing as it nears its source
Of motion—by which law all things so'er
Are clutch'd and dragg'd and held—so fell she there,
Like a dead stone, down in her headlong course.

28

The disregardful silence heard her strike
Upon the solid crags; her dismal shriek
Rang on the rocks and died out laughter-like
Along the vale in hurried trebles weak;
And soon upon her, from their skiey haunt
Fell to their feast the great birds bald and gaunt,
And gorged on her fair flesh with bloody beak.

29

But Psyche, when her sister was gone forth,
Went out again her wandering way to take:
And following a stream that led her north,
After some days she pass'd the Corian Lake,
Whereby Athena's temple stands, and he
Who traverses the isle from sea to sea
May by the plain his shortest journey make:

30

Till on the northern coast arrived she came
Upon a city built about a port,
The which she knew, soon as she heard the name,

Was where her eldest sister held her court ;
To whom, as Eros had commanded her,
She now in turn became the messenger
Of vengeful punishment, that fell not short:

31

For she too hearing gan her heart exalt,
Nor pity felt for Psyche's tears and moans,
But, fellow'd with that other in her fault,
Follow'd her to her fate upon the stones;
And from the peak leaping like her below
The self-same way unto the self-same woe,
Lay dasht to death upon her sister's bones.

THIRD QUARTER

Autumn

Psyche's wanderings.

SEPTEMBER

I

ON the Hellenic board of Crete's fair isle,
   Westward of Drepanon, along a reach
Which massy Cyamum for many a mile
Jutting to sea delivers from the breach
Of North and East,—returning to embay
The favour'd shore—an ancient city lay,
Aptera, which is *Wingless* in our speech.

.

2

And hence the name; that here in rocky cove,
Thence called Museion, was the trial waged
What day the Sirens with the Muses strove,
By jealous Hera in that war engaged:
Wherein the daughters of Mnemosynè
O'ercame the chauntresses who vex'd the sea,
Nor vengeance spared them by their pride enraged.

3

For those strange creatures, who with women's words
And wiles made ravenous prey of passers-by,
Were throated with the liquid pipe of birds:
Of love they sang; and none, who sail'd anigh
Through the grey hazes of the cyanine sea,
Had wit the whirlpool of that song to flee,
Nor fear'd the talon hook'd and feather'd thigh.

4

But them the singers of the gods o'ercame,
And pluck'd them of their plumage, where in fright
They vainly flutter'd off to hide their shame,
Upon two rocks that lie within the bight,
Under the headland, barren and alone;
Which, being with the scatter'd feathers strewn,
Were, by the folk named Leukæ, which is *White*.

5

Thereon about this time the snowy gull,
Minion of Aphrodite, being come,
Plumed himself, standing on the sea-wrack dull,   .

That drifted from the foot of Cyamum;
And 'twas his thought, that had the goddess learnt
The tale of Psyche loved and Eros burnt,
She ne'er so long had kept aloof and dumb.

6

Wherefore that duteous gossip of Love's queen
Devised that he the messenger would be;
And rising from the rock, he skim'd between
The chasing waves—such grace have none but he;—
Into the middle deep then down he dived,
And rowing with his glistening wings, arrived
At Aphrodite's bower beneath the sea.

7

The eddies from his silver pinions swirl'd
The crimson, green, and yellow floss, that grew
About the caves, and at his passing curl'd
Its graceful silk, and gently waved anew:
Till, oaring here and there, the queen he found
Stray'd from her haunt unto a sandy ground,
Dappl'd with eye-rings in the sunlight blue.

8

She, as he came upon her from above,
With Hora play'd; Hora, her herald fair,
That lays the soft necessity of Love
On maidens' eyelids, and with tender care
Marketh the hour, as in all works is fit:
And happy they in love who time outwit,
Fondly constrainèd in her season rare.

9

But he with garrulous and laughing tongue
Broke up his news; how Eros, fallen sick,
Lay tossing on his bed, to frenzy stung
By such a burn as did but barely prick:
A little bleb, no bigger than a pease,
Upon his shoulder 'twas, that kill'd his ease,
Fever'd his heart, and made his breathing thick.

10

"For which disaster hath he not been seen
This many a day at all in any place:
And thou, dear mistress," piped he, "hast not been

Thyself amongst us now a dreary space :
The pining mortals suffer from a dearth
Of love ; and for this sadness of the earth
Thy family is darken'd with disgrace.

11

"Now on the secret paths of dale and wood,
Where lovers walk'd are lovers none to find :
And friends, besworn to equal brotherhood,
Forget their faith, and part with words unkind :
In the first moon thy honey bond is loath'd :
And I could tell even of the new-betroth'd
That fly o'ersea, and leave their loves behind.

12

"Summer is over, but the merry pipe,
That wont to cheer the harvesting, is mute :
And in the vineyards, where the grape is ripe,
No voice is heard of them that take the fruit.
No workman singeth at eve nor maiden danceth :
All joy is dead, and as the year advanceth
The signs of woe increase on man and brute.

13

"'Tis plain that if thy pleasure longer pause,
Thy mighty rule on earth hath seen its day:
The race must come to perish, and no cause
But that thou sittest with thy nymphs at play,
While on a Cretan hill thy truant boy
Hath with his pretty mistress turn'd to toy,
And less for pain than love pineth away."

14

"Ha! Mistress!" cried she; "Hath my beardless son
Been hunting for himself his lovely game?
Some young Orestiad hath his fancy won?
Some Naiad? say; or is a Grace his flame?
Or maybe Muse, and then 'tis Erato,
The trifling wanton.   Tell me, if thou know,
Woman or goddess is she? and her name."

15

Then said the snowy gull, "O heavenly queen,
What is my knowledge, who am but a bird?
Yet is she only mortal, as I ween,

And naméd Psyche, if I rightly heard."—
But Aphrodite's look daunted his cheer,
Ascare he fled away, screaming in fear,
To see what wrath his simple tale had stirr'd.

16

He flasht his pens, and sweeping widely round
Tower'd to air ; so swift in all his way,
That whence he dived he there again was found
As soon as if he had but dipt for prey :
And now, or e'er he join'd his wailful flock,
Once more he stood upon the Sirens' rock,
And preen'd his ruffl'd quills for fresh display.

17

But as ill tidings have their truth assured
Without more witness than their fatal sense,
So, since was nought she less could have endured,
The injured goddess guess'd the full offence :
And doubted only whether first to smite
Or Psyche for her new presumptuous flight,
Or Eros for his disobedience.

18

But full of anger to her son she went,
And found him in his golden chamber laid;
And with him sweet Euphrosynè, attent
Upon his murmur'd wants, aye as he bade
Shifted the pillows with each fretful whim;
But scornfully his mother look'd at him,
And reckless of his pain gan thus upbraid:

19

"O worthy deeds, I say, and true to blood,
The crown and pledge of promise! thou that wast
In estimation my perpetual bud,
Now fruiting thus untimely to my cost;
Backsliding from commandment, ay, and worse,
With bliss to favour one I bade thee curse,
And save the life I left with thee for lost!

20

"Thou too to burn with love, and love of her
Whom I did hate; and to thy bed to take
My rival, that my trusted officer

Might of mine enemy my daughter make!
Dost thou then think my love for thee so fond,
And miserably doting, that the bond
By such dishonour strainèd will not break?

21

"Or that I cannot bear another son
As good as thou; or, if I choose not bear,
Not beg as good a lusty boy of one
Of all my nymphs,—and some have boys to spare,—
One I might train, to whom thine arms made o'er
Should do me kinder service than before,
To smite my foes and keep my honour fair?

22

"For thou hast ever mockt me, and beguiled
In amours strange my God, thy valiant sire:
And having smirch'd our fame while yet a child
Wilt further foul it now with earthly fire.
But I—do as thou may—have vow'd to kill
Thy fancied girl, whether thou love her still,
Or of her silly charms already tire.

23

"Tell me but where she hides."   And Eros now,
Proud in his woe, boasted his happy theft :
Confessing he had loved her well, and how
By her own doing she was lost and left;
And homeless in such sorrow as outwent
The utmost pain of other punishment,
Was wandering of his love and favour reft.

24

By which was Cypris gladden'd, not appeased,
But hid her joy and spake no more her threat :
And left with face like one that much displeased
First bending deigns a sign he may forget.
    When lo! as swiftly she came stepping down
From her fair house into the heavenly town
The Kronian sisters on the way she met;

25

Hera, the Wife of Zeus, her placid front
Dark with the shadow of his troubl'd reign,
And tall Demeter, who with men once wont,

Holding the high Olympians in disdain
For Persephassa's rape; which now forgiven,
She had return'd unto the courts of Heaven,
And 'mong the immortals liv'd at peace again:

26

Whose smile told Aphrodite that they knew
The meaning of her visit; and a flush
Of anger answer'd them, while hot she grew.
But Hera laugh'd outright: "Why thou dost blush!
Now see we modest manners on my life!
And all thy little son has got a wife
Can make the crimson to thy forehead rush.

27

"Didst think he, whom thou madest passion's prince,
No privy dart then for himself would poise?
Nay, by the cuckoo on my sceptre, since
'Twas love that made thee mother of his joys,
Art thou the foremost to his favour bound;
As thou shouldst be the last to think to sound
The heart, and least of all thy wanton boy's."

H

28

But her Demeter, on whose stalwart arm
She lean'd, took up : "If thou wilt hark to me,
This Psyche," said she, "hath the heavenly charm,
And will become immortal.   And maybe
To marry with a woman is as well
As wed a god and live below in Hell :
As 'twas my lot in child of mine to see."

29

Which things they both said, fearing in their hearts
That savage Eros, if they mockt his case,
Would kill their peace with his revengeful darts,
And bring them haply to a worse disgrace :
But Aphrodite, saying "Good ! my dames ;
Behind this smoke I see the spite that flames,"
Left them, and on her journey went apace.

30

For having purposed she would hold no truce
With Psyche or her son, 'twas in her mind
To go forthwith unto the throne of Zeus,

SEPTEMBER

And beg that Hermes might be sent to find
The wanderer; and secure that in such quest
He would not fail, she ponder'd but how best
She might inflict her vengeance long-design'd.

OCTOBER

1

HEAVY meanwhile at heart, with bruisèd feet
    Was Psyche wandering many nights and days
Upon the paths of hundred-citied Crete,
And chose to step the most deserted ways;
Being least unhappy when she went unseen;
Since else her secret sorrow had no screen
From the plain question of men's idle gaze.

2

Yet wheresoe'er she went one hope she had;
Like mortal mourners, who 'gainst reason strong
Hope to be unexpectedly made glad
With sight of their dead friends, so much they long;
So she for him, whom loss a thousandfold
Endear'd and made desired; nor could she hold
He would not turn and quite forgive her wrong.

3

Wherefore her eager eyes in every place
Lookt for her lover; and 'twixt hope and fear
She follow'd oft afar some form of grace,
In pain alike to lose or venture near.
And still this thought cheer'd her fatigue, that he,
Or on some hill, or by some brook or tree,
But waited for her coming to appear.

4

And then for comfort many an old love-crost
And doleful ditty would she gently sing,
Writ by sad poets of a lover lost,
Now sounding sweeter for her sorrowing:
Echo, sweet Echo, watching up on high,
Say hast thou seen to-day my love go by,
Or where thou sittest by thy mossy spring?

5

Or say ye nymphs, that from the crystal rills,
When ye have bathed your limbs from morn till eve,
Flying at midnight to the bare-topt hills,

Beneath the stars your mazy dances weave,
Say, my deserter, whom ye well may know
By his small wings, his quiver, and his bow,
Say, have ye seen my love, whose loss I grieve?

6

Till climb'd one evening on a rocky steep
Above the plain of Cisamos, that lay,
Robb'd of its golden harvest, in the deep
Mountainous shadows of the dying day,
She saw a temple, whose tall columns fair
Recall'd her home; and "O if thou be there,
My love," she cried, "fly not again away."

7

Swiftly she ran, and entering by the door
She stood alone within an empty fane
Of great Demeter: and, behold, the floor
Was litter'd with thank-offerings of grain,
With wheat and barley-sheaves together heapt
In holy harvest-home of them that reapt
The goddess' plenteous gifts upon the plain;

8

And on the tithe the tackle of the tithe
Thrown by in such confusion, as are laid
Upon the swath sickle, and hook, and scythe,
When midday drives the reapers to the shade.
And Psyche, since had come no priestess there
To trim the temple, in her pious care
Forgat herself, and lent her duteous aid.

9

She drew the offerings from the midst aside,
And piled the sheaves at every pillar's base;
And sweeping therebetween a passage wide,
Made clear of corn and chaff the temple space:
As countrymen who bring their wheat to mart,
Set out their show along the walls apart
By their allotted stations, each in place;

10

Thus she, and felt no weariness,—such strength
Hath duty to support our feeble frame,—
Till all was set in order, and at length

Up to the threshold of the shrine she came :
When lo ! before her face with friendly smile,
Tall as a pillar of the peristyle,
The goddess stood reveal'd, and call'd her name.

11

" Unhappy Psyche," said she, " know'st thou not
How Aphrodite to thy hurt is sworn ?
And thou, thy peril and her wrath forgot,
Spendest thy thought my temple to adorn.
Take better heed ! "—And Psyche, at the voice
Even of so little comfort, gan rejoice,
And at her feet pour'd out this prayer forlorn.

12

" O Gracious giver of the golden grain,
Hide me, I pray thee, from her wrath unkind ;
For who can pity as canst thou my pain,
Who wert thyself a wanderer, vex'd in mind
For loss of thy dear Corè once, whenas,
Ravisht to hell by fierce Agesilas,
Thou soughtest her on earth and coudst not find.

13

"How coud thy feet bear thee to western night,
And where swart Libyans watch the sacred tree,
And thrice to ford o'er Achelous bright,
And all the streams of beauteous Sicily?
And thrice to Enna cam'st thou, thrice, they tell,
Satest athirst by Callichorus' well,
Nor tookest of the spring to comfort thee.

14

"By that remember'd anguish of thine heart,
Lady, have pity even on me, and show
Where I may find my love; and take my part
For peace, I pray, against my cruel foe:
Or if thou canst not from her anger shield,
Here let me lie among the sheaves conceal'd
Such time till forth I may in safety go."

15

Demeter answer'd, "Nay, though thou constrain
My favour with thy plea, my help must still
Be hidden, else I work for thee in vain

To thwart my mighty sister in her will.
Thou must fly hence: Yet though I not oppose,
Less will I aid her; and if now I close
My temple doors to thee, take it not ill."

16

Then Psyche's hope founder'd; as when a ship,
The morrow of the gale can hardly ride
The swollen seas, fetching a deeper dip
At every wave, and through her gaping side
And o'er her shattered bulwark ever drinks,
Till plunging in the watery wild she sinks,
To scoop her grave beneath the crushing tide:

17

So with each word her broken spirit drank
Its doom; and overwhelm'd with deep despair
She turn'd away, and coming forth she sank
Silently weeping on the temple stair,
In midmost night, forspent with long turmoil:
But sleep, the gracious pursuivant of toil,
Came swiftly down, and nursed away her care.

18

And when the sun awaked her with his beams
She found new hope, that still her sorrow's cure
Lay with the gods, who in her morning dreams
Had sent her comfort in a vision sure;
Wherein the Cretan-born, almightiest god,
Cloud-gathering Zeus himself had seem'd to nod,
And bid her with good heart her woes endure.

19

So coming that same day unto a shrine
Of Hera, she took courage and went in:
And like to one that to the cell divine
For favour ventures or a suit to win,
She drew anigh the altar, from her face
Wiping the tears, ere to the heavenly grace,
As thus she pray'd, she would her prayer begin.

20

" Most honour'd Lady, who from ancient doom
Wert made heaven's wife, and art on earth besought
With gracious happiness of all to whom

Thy holy wedlock hath my burden brought,
Save me from Aphrodite's fell pursuit,
And guard unto the birth Love's hapless fruit,
Which she for cruel spite would bring to nought.

21

"As once from her thou wert not shamed to take
Her beauty's zone, thy beauty to enhance;
For which again Zeus loved thee, to forsake
His warlike ire in faithful dalliance;
Show me what means may win my Love to me,
Or how that I may come, if so may be,
Within the favour of his countenance.

22

"If there be any place for tears or prayer,
If there be need for succour in distress,
Now is the very hour of all despair,
Here is the heart of grief and bitterness.
Motherly pity, bend thy face and grant
One beam of ruth to thy poor suppliant,
Nor turn me from thine altar comfortless."

23

Even as she pray'd a cloud spread through the cell,
And 'mid the wreathings of the vapour dim
The goddess grew in glory visible,
Like some barbaric queen in festal trim;
Such the attire and ornaments she wore,
When o'er the forgèd threshold of the floor
Of Zeus's house she stept to visit him.

24

From either ear, ring'd to its piercèd lobe
A triple jewel hung, with gold enchas't;
And o'er her breasts her wide ambrosial robe
With many a shining golden clasp was brac't;
The flowering on its smooth embroider'd lawn
Gather'd to colour where the zone was drawn
In fringe of golden tassels at her waist.

25

Her curling hair with plaited braid and brail,
Pendant or loop'd about her head divine,
Lay hidden half beneath a golden veil,

Bright as the rippling ocean in sunshine :
And on the ground, flashing whene'er she stept,
Beneath her feet the dazzling lightnings lept
From the gold network of her sandals fine.

26

Thus Hera stood in royal guise bedeckt
Before poor Psyche on the stair that knelt,
Whose new-nursed hope at that display was checkt,
And all her happier thoughts gan fade and melt.
She saw no kindness in such haughty mien,
And venturing not to look upon the queen,
Bow'd down in woe to hear her sentence dealt.

27

And thus the goddess spake, "In vain thou suest,
Most miserable Psyche; though my heart
Be full of hate for her whose hate thou ruest,
And pride and pity move me to thy part:
Yet not till Zeus make known his will, coud I,
Least of the blameless gods that dwell on high,
Assist thee, wert thou worthier than thou art.

28

" But know if Eros love thee, that thy hopes
Should rest on him; and I would bid thee go
Where in his mother's house apart he mopes
Grieving for loss of thee in secret woe:
For should he take thee back, there is no power
In earth or heaven will hurt thee from that hour,
Nay, not if Zeus himself should prove thy foe."

29

   Thus saying she was gone, and Psyche now
Surprised by comfort rose and went her way,
Resolved in heart, and only wondering how
'Twas possible to come where Eros lay;
Since that her feet, however she might roam,
Could never travel to the heavenly home
Of Love, beyond the bounds of mortal day :

30

Yet must she come to him.   And now 'twas proved
How that to Lovers, as is told in song,
Seeking the way no place is far removed;

Nor is there any obstacle so strong,
Nor bar so fix'd that it can hinder them :
And how to reach heaven's gate by stratagem
Vex'd not the venturous heart of Psyche long.

31

To face her enemy might well avail :
Wherefore to Cypris' shrine her steps she bent,
Hoping the goddess in her hate might hale
Her body to the skies for punishment,
Whate'er to be ; yet now her fiercest wrath
Seemed happiest fortune, seeing 'twas the path
Whereby alone unto her love she went.

NOVEMBER

1

BUT Aphrodite to the house of Zeus
  Being bound, bade beckon out her milkwhite
    steeds,
Four doves, that ready to her royal use
In golden cages stood and peck'd the seeds :
Best of the hundred prison'd birds she broke,
That wore with pride the marking of her yoke,
And cooed in envy of her gentle needs.

2

These drew in turn her chariot, when in state
Along the heaven with all her train she fared;
And oft in journeying to the skiey gate
Of Zeus's palace high their flight had dared,
Which darkest vapour and thick glooms enshroud
Above all else in the perpetual cloud,
Wherethro' to mount again they stood prepared,

3

Sleeking their feathers, by her shining car;
  The same Hephæstos wrought for her, when he,
Bruised in his hideous fall from heaven afar,
Was nursed by Thetis, and Eurynomè,
The daughter of the ever-refluent main;
With whom he dwelt till he grew sound again,
Down in a hollow cave beside the sea:

4

And them for kindness done was prompt to serve,
Forging them brooches rich in make and mode,
Earrings, and supple chains of jointed curve,
And other trinkets, while he there abode:
And none of gods or men knew of his home,
But they two only; and the salt sea-foam
To and fro past his cavern ever flow'd.

5

'Twas then he wrought this work within the cave,
Emboss'd with rich design, a moonèd car;
And when returned to heaven to Venus gave,

In form imagined like her crescent star;
Which circling nearest earth, maketh at night
To wakeful mortal men shadow and light
Alone of all the stars in heaven that are.

6

Two slender wheels it had, with fretted tires
Of biting adamant, to take firm hold
Of cloud or ether; and their whirling fires
Threw off the air in halo where they roll'd :
And either nave that round the axle turn'd
A ruby was, whose steady crimson burn'd
Betwixt the twin speed-mingling fans of gold.

7

Thereon the naked goddess mounting shook
The reins; whereat the doves their wings outspread,
And rising high their flight to heaven they took :
And all the birds, that in those courts were bred,
Of her broad eaves the nested families,
Sparrows and swallows join'd their companies
Awhile and twitter'd to her overhead.

8

But onward she with fading tracks of flame
Sped swiftly, till she reacht her journey's end:
And when within the house of Zeus she came,
She pray'd the Sire of Heaven that he would lend
Hermes, the Argus-slayer, for her hest;
And he being granted her at her request,
She went forthwith to seek him and to send.

9

Who happ'd within the palace then to wait
Upon the almighty pleasure; and her tale
Was quickly told, and he made answer straight
That he would find the truant without fail;
Asking the goddess by what signs her slave
Might best be known, and what the price she gave
For capture, or admitted for the bail.

10

All which he took his silver stile to write
In letters large upon a waxèd board;
Her age and name, her colour, face and height,

Her home, and parentage, and the reward:
And then read o'er as 'twas to be proclaim'd.
And she took oath to give the price she named,
Without demur, when Psyche was restored.

11

Then on his head he closely set his cap
With earèd wings erect, and o'er his knee
He cross'd each foot in turn to prove the strap
That bound his wingèd sandals, and shook free
His chlamys, and gat up, and in his hand
Taking his fair white-ribbon'd herald's wand,
Lept forth on air, accoutred cap-a-pè.

12

And piloting along the mid-day sky,
Held southward, till the narrow map of Crete
Lay like a fleck in azure 'neath his eye;
When down he came, and as an eagle fleet
Drops in some combe, then checks his headlong stoop
With wide-flung wing, wheeling in level swoop
To strike the bleating quarry with his feet,

13

Thus he alighted ; and in every town
In all the isle before the close of day
Had cried the message, which he carried down,
Of Psyche, Aphrodite's runaway ;
That whosoever found the same and caught,
And by such time unto her temple brought,
To him the goddess would this guerdon pay :

14

SIX HONIED KISSES FROM HER ROSY MOUTH
WOULD CYTHEREA GIVE, AND ONE BESIDE
TO QUENCH AT HEART FOR AYE LOVE'S MORTAL DROUTH :
BUT UNTO HIM THAT HID HER, WOE BETIDE !
Which now was on all tongues, and Psyche's name
Herself o'erheard, or ever nigh she came
To Aphrodite's temple where she hied.

15

When since she found her way to heaven was safe,
She only wisht to make it soon and sure ;
Nor fear'd to meet the goddess in her chafe,

So she her self-surrender might secure,
And not be given of other for the price ;
Nor was there need of any artifice
Her once resplendent beauty to obscure.

16

For now so changed she was by heavy woe,
That for the little likeness that she bore
To her description she was fear'd to go
Within the fane ; and when she stood before
The priestess, scarce coud she with oath persuade
That she was Psyche, the renownèd maid,
Whom men had left the temple to adore.

17

But when to Hermes she was shown and given,
He took no doubt, but eager to be on it,
And proud of speed, return'd with her to heaven,
And left her with the proclamation writ,
Hung at her neck, the board with letters large,
At Aphrodite's gate with those in charge ;
And up whence first he came made haste to flit.

18

But hapless Psyche fell, for so it chanced,
To moody SYNETHEA's care, the one
Of Aphrodite's train whom she advanced
To try the work abandon'd by her son.
Who by perpetual presence made ill end
Of good or bad; though she could both amend,
And merit praise for work by her begun.

19

But she to better thought her heart had shut,
And proved she had a spite beyond compare:
Nor could the keenest taunts her anger glut,
Which she when sour'd was never wont to spare:
And now she mock'd at Psyche's shame and grief,
As only she might do, and to her chief
Along the courtyard dragg'd her by the hair.

20

Nor now was Aphrodite kinder grown:
Having her hated rival in her power,
She laught for joy, and in triumphant tone

Bade her a merry welcome to her bower :
"'Tis fit indeed daughters-in-law should wait
Upon their mothers ; but thou comest late,
Psyche ; I lookt for thee before this hour.

21

" And yet," thus gave she rein to jeer and gibe,
" Forgive me if I held thee negligent,
Or if accustom'd vanity ascribe
An honour to myself that was not meant.
Thy lover is it, who so dearly prized
The pretty soul, then left her and despised ?
To him more like thy heavenward steps were bent :

22

" Nor without reason : Zeus, I tell thee, swoon'd
To hear the story of the drop of oil,
The revelation and the ghastly wound :
My merriment is but my fear's recoil.
But if my son was unkind, thou shalt see
How kind a goddess can his mother be
To bring thy tainted honour clear of soil."

23

And so, to match her promise with her mirth,
Two of her ministers she call'd in ken,
That work the melancholy of the earth;
MERIMNA that with care perplexes, when
The hearts of mortals have the gods forgot,
And LYPÈ, that her sorrow spares them not,
When mortals have forgot their fellow men.

24

These, like twin sharks that in a fair ship's wake
Swim constant, showing 'bove the water blue
Their shearing fins, and hasty ravin make
Of overthrow. or offal, so these two
On Aphrodite's passing follow hard;
And now she offer'd to their glut's regard
Sweet Psyche, with command their wont to do.

25

But in what secret chamber their foul task
These soul-tormentors plied, or what their skill,
Pity of tender nature may not ask, ·

Nor poet stain his rhyme with such an ill.
But they at last themselves turn'd from their rack,
Weary of cruelty, and led her back,
Saying that further torture were to kill.

26

Then when the goddess saw her, more she mockt,
"Art thou the woman of the earth," she said,
"That hast in sorceries mine Eros lockt,
And stood thyself for worship in my stead?
Looking that I should pity thee, or care
For what illicit offspring thou mayst bear;
Or let thee to that god my son be wed?

27

"I know thy trick; and thou art one of them
Who steal love's favour in the gentle way,
Wearing submission for a diadem,
Patience and suffering for thy rich array:
Thou wilt be modest, kind, implicit, so
To rest thy wily spirit out of show
That it may leap the livelier into play:

28

"Devout at doing nothing, if so be
The grace become thee well; but active yet
Above all others be there none to see
Thy business, and thine eager face asweat.
Lo ! I will prove thy talent: thou mayst live,
And all thou now desirest will I give,
If thou perform the task which I shall set."

29

She took her then aside, and bade her heed
A heap of grains piled high upon the floor,
Millet and mustard, hemp and poppy seed,
And fern-bloom's undistinguishable spore,
All kinds of pulse, of grasses, and of spice,
Clover and linseed, rape, and corn, and rice,
Dodder, and sesame, and many more.

30

"Sort me these seeds" she said; "it now is night,
I will return at morning; if I find
That thou hast separated all aright,

Each grain from other grain after its kind,
And set them in unmingl'd heaps apart,
Then shall thy wish be granted to thine heart."
Whereat she turn'd, and closed the door behind.

FOURTH QUARTER
Winter

Psyche's trials and reception into heaven.

DECEMBER

1

A SINGLE lamp there stood beside the heap,
And shed thereon its mocking golden light;
Such as might tempt the weary eye to sleep
Rather than prick the nerve of taskèd sight.
Yet Psyche, not to fail for lack of zeal,
With good will sat her down to her ordeal,.
Sorting the larger seeds as best she might.

2

When lo! upon the wall, a shadow past
Of doubtful shape, across the chamber dim
Moving with speed: and seeing nought that cast
The shade, she bent her down the flame to trim;
And there the beast itself, a little ant,
Climb'd up in compass of the lustre scant,
Upon the bowl of oil ran round the rim.

3

Smiling to see the creature of her fear
So dwarf'd by truth, she watcht him where he crept,
For mere distraction telling in his ear
What straits she then was in, and telling wept.
Whereat he stood and trim'd his horns; but ere
Her tale was done resumed his manner scare,
Ran down, and on his way in darkness kept.

4

But she intent drew forth with dextrous hand
The larger seeds, or push'd the smaller back,
Or light from heavy with her breathing fan'd.
When suddenly she saw the floor grow black,
And troops of ants, flowing in noiseless train,
Moved to the hill of seeds, as o'er a plain
Armies approach a city for attack;

5

And gathering on the grain, began to strive
With grappling horns: and each from out the heap
His burden drew, and all their motion live

Struggled and slid upon the surface steep.
And Psyche wonder'd, watching them, to find
The creatures separated kind from kind:
Till dizzied with the sight she fell asleep.

6

And when she woke 'twas with the morning sound
Of Aphrodite's anger at the door,
Whom high amaze stay'd backward, as she found
Her foe asleep with all her trouble o'er:
And round the room beheld, in order due,
The piles arranged distinct and sorted true,
Grain with grain, seed with seed, and spore with
    spore.

7

She fiercely cried " Thou shalt not thus escape;
For to this marvel dar'st thou not pretend.
There is but one that could this order shape,
Demeter,—but I knew her not thy friend.
Therefore another trial will I set,
In which she cannot aid thee nor abet,
But thou thyself must bring it fair to end."

8

Thereon she sped her to the bounds of Thrace,
And set her by a river deep and wide,
And said "To east beyond this stream, a race
Of golden-fleecèd sheep at pasture bide.
Go seek them out; and this thy task, to pull
But one lock for me of their precious wool,
And give it in my hands at eventide:

9

"This do and thou shalt have thy heart's desire."
Which said, she fled and left her by the stream:
And Psyche then, with courage still entire
Had plunged therein; but now of great esteem
Her life she rated, while it lent a spell
Wherein she yet might hope to quit her well,
And in one winning all her woes redeem.

10

There as she stood in doubt, a fluting voice
Rose from the flood, "Psyche, be not afraid
To hear a reed give tongue, for 'twas of choice

That I from mortal flesh a plant was made.
My name is Syrinx; once from mighty Pan
Into the drowning river as I ran,
A fearful prayer my steps for ever stay'd.

11

"But by that change in many climes I live;
And Pan, my lover, who to me alone
Is true and does me honour, I forgive—
Nor if I speak in sorrow is't my own:
Rather for thee my voice I now uplift
To warn thee plunge not in the river swift,
Nor seek the golden sheep to men unknown.

12

"If thou should cross the stream, which may not be
Thou coudst not climb upon the hanging rocks,
Nor ever, as the goddess bade thee, see
The pasture of the yellow-fleecèd flocks:
Or if thou coud, their herded horns would gore
And slay thee on the crags, or thrust thee o'er
Ere thou coudst rob them of their golden locks.

13

"The goddess means thy death.   But I can show
How thy obedience yet may thwart her will.
At noon the golden flocks descend below,
Leaving the scented herbage of the hill,
And where the shelving banks to shallows fall,
Drink at the rippling water one and all,
Nor back return till they have drawn their fill.

14

"I will command a thornbush, that it stoop
Over some ram that steppeth by in peace,
And him in all its prickles firmly coop,
Making thee seizure of his golden fleece;
So without peril of his angry horns
Shalt thou be quit: for he upon the thorns
Must leave his ransom ere he win release."

15

Then Psyche thankt her for her kind befriending,
And hid among the rushes looking east;
And when noon came she saw the flock descending

Out of the hills; and lo! one golden beast
Caught in a thornbush; and the mighty brute
Struggl'd and tore it from its twisted root
Into the stream, or e'er he was releas't.

16

And when they water'd were and gone, the breeze
Floated the freighted thorn where Psyche lay :
Whence she unhook'd the golden wool at ease,
And back to heaven for passage swift gan pray.
And Hermes, who was sent to be her guide
Ifso she lived, came down at eventide,
And bore her thither ere the close of day.

17

But when the goddess saw the locks of gold
Held to her hands, her heart with wrath o'erran :
"Most desperate thou, and by abetting bold,
That dost outwit me, prove thee as I can.
Yet this work is not thine : there is but one
Of all the gods who coud the thing have done.
Hast thou a friend too in the lusty Pan ?

18

"I'll give thee trial where he cannot aid."
  Which said, she led her to a torrid land,
Level and black, but not with flood or shade,
For nothing coud the mighty heat withstand,
Which aye from morn till eve the naked sun
Pour'd on that plain, where never foot had run,
Nor any herb sprung on its mólten sand.

19

Far off a gloomy mountain rose alone :
And Aphrodite, thither pointing, said
"There lies thy task.   Out of the topmost stone
Of yonder hill upwells a fountain head.
Take thou this goblet; brimming must thou bring
Its cup with water from that sacred spring,
If ever to my son thou wouldst be wed."

20

Saying, she gave into her hands a bowl
Cut of one crystal, open, broad and fair ;
And bade her at all hazard keep it whole,

For heaven held nought beside so fine or rare.
Then was she gone; and Psyche on the plain
Now doubted if she ever should regain
The love of Eros, strove she howsoe'er.

21

Yet as a helmsman, at the word to tack,
Swiftly without a thought puts down his helm,
So Psyche turn'd to tread that desert black,
Since was no fear that coud her heart o'erwhelm;
Nor knew she that the fount she went to seek
Was cold Cocytus, springing to the peak,
Secretly from his source in Pluto's realm.

22

All night and day she journey'd, and at last
Come to the rock gazed up in vain around:
Nothing she saw but precipices vast
O'er ruined scarps, with rugged ridges crown'd:
And creeping to a cleft to rest in shade,
Or e'er the desperate venture she assay'd,
She fell asleep upon the stony ground.

23

A dream came to her, thus : she stood alone
Within her palace in the high ravine ;
Where nought but she was changed, but she to stone.
Worshippers throng'd the court, and still were seen
Folk flying from the peak, who, ever more
Flying and flying, lighted on the floor,
Hail! cried they, *wife of Eros, adorèd queen!*

24

A hurtling of the battl'd air disturb'd
Her sunken sense, and waked her eyes to meet
The kingly bird of Zeus, himself that curb'd
His swooping course, alighting at her feet ;
With motion gentle, his far-darting eye
In kindness dim'd upon her, he drew nigh,
And thus in words unveil'd her foe's deceit :

25

" In vain, poor Psyche, hast thou hither striven
Across the fiery plain toiling so well ;
Cruelly to destruction art thou driven

By her, whose hate thou canst not quit nor quell.
No mortal foot may scale this horrid mount,
And those black waters of its topmost fount
Are guarded by the hornèd snakes of hell.

26

" Its little rill is an upleaping jet
Of cold Cocytus, which for ever licks
Earth's base, and when with Acheron 'tis met,
Its waters with that other cannot mix,
Which holds the elemental air dissolved;
But with it in its ceaseless course revolved
Issues unmingl'd in the lake of Styx.

27

" The souls of murderers, in guise of fish,
Scream as they swim therein and wail or cold,
Their times of woe determined by the wish
Of them they murder'd on the earth of old:
Whom each five years they see, whene'er they make
Their passage on the Acherusian lake,
And there release may win from pains condoled.

28

"For if the pitying ear of them they slew
Be haply piercèd by their voices spare,
Then are they freed from pain ; as are some few ;
But, for the most, again they forward fare
To Tartarus obscene, and outcast thence
Are hurried back into the cold intense,
And with new company their torments share.

29

"Its biting lymph may not be touch'd of man
Or god, unless the Fates have so ordain'd ;
Nor coud I in thy favour break the ban,
Nor pass the dragons that thereby are chain'd,
Didst thou not bear the sacred cup of Zeus ;
Which, for thy peril lent, shall turn to use,
And truly do the service which it feign'd."

30

Thus as he spake, his talons made he ring
Around the crystal bowl, and soaring high
Descended as from heaven upon the spring :

Nor dared the hornèd snakes of hell deny
The minister of Zeus, that bore his cup,
To fill it with their trusted water up,
Thence to the King of heaven therewith to fly.

31

But he to Psyche bent his gracious speed,
And bidding her to mount his feather'd back
Bore her aloft as once young Ganymede;
Nor ever made his steady flight to slack,
Ere that he set her down beside her goal,
And gave into her hands the crystal bowl
Unspill'd, o'erbrimming with the water black.

JANUARY

1

BUT Eros now recover'd from his hurt,
 Felt other pangs; for who would not relent
Weighing the small crime and unmatch'd desert
Of Psyche with her cruel punishment?
And shamed he grew to be so near allied
To her, who by her taunts awoke his pride,
As his compassion by her spite unspent.

2

Which Aphrodite seeing, wax'd more firm
That he should never meet with Psyche more;
And had in thought already set the term
To their communion with that trial sore,
Which sent her forth upon a quest accurst,
And not to be accomplisht, that of thirst
She there might perish on hell's torrid shore.

3

And now it chanced that she had called her son
Into her presence-chamber, to unfold
Psyche's destruction, that her fate might stun
What love remained by duty uncontrol'd;
And he to hide his tears' rebellious storm
Was fled; when in his place another form
Rose 'neath the golden lintel; and behold

4

Psyche herself, in slow and balanced strain,
Poising the crystal bowl with fearful heed,
Her eyes at watch upon the steadied plane,
And whole soul gather'd in the single deed.
Onward she came, and stooping to the floor
Set down the cup unspill'd and brimming o'er
At Aphrodite's feet, and rose up freed.

5

Surprise o'ercame the goddess, and she too
Stood like a statue, but with passion pale:
Till, when her victim nothing spake, she threw

Some kindness in her voice, and bade her hail;
But in the smiling judge 'twas plain to see—
Saying "What water bringst thou here to me?"—
That justice over hate should not prevail.

6

Then Psyche said "This is the biting flood
Of black Cocytus, silver'd with the gleam
Of souls, that guilty of another's blood
Are pent therein, and as they swim they scream.
The hornèd snakes of hell, upon the mount
Enchain'd, for ever guard the livid fount:
And but the Fates can grant to touch the stream."

7

"Wherefore," the goddess cried, "'tis plain that none
But one I wot of coud this thing have wrought.
That which another doth may well be done,
Nor thou the nearer to my promise brought.
Thou buildest on a hope to be destroy'd,
If thou accept conditions, and avoid
Thy parcel, nor thyself accomplish aught.

8

"Was it not kindness in me, being averse
To all thy wish, to yield me thus to grant
Thy heart's desire,—and nothing loathe I worse,—
If thou wouldst only work as well as want?
See, now I will not yet be all denial,
But offer thee one last determining trial;
And let it be a mutual covenant:

9

"This box," and in her hands she took a pyx
Square-cut, of dark obsidian's rarest green,
"Take; and therewith beyond Tartarean Styx
Go thou, and entering Hades' house obscene,
Say to Persephonè, *If 'tis thy will*
To shew me so much favour, prithee fill
This little vase with beauty for Love's queen.

10

"*She begs but what shall well o'erlast a day:*
For of her own was much of late outspent
In nursing of her son, in bed who lay

L

Wounded by me, who for the gift am sent.
Then bring me what she gives, and with all speed;
For truth to say I stand, thou seest, in need
Of some such charm in my disparagement.

11

" If thou return to me with that acquist,
Having thyself the journey made, I swear
That day to give thee whatsoe'er thou list,
An be it my son.   Now, Psyche, wilt thou dare? "
And Psyche said " If this thou truly mean,
I will go down to Tartarus obscene,
And beg of Hades' queen thy beauty there.

12

" Show me the way."   But Aphrodite said,
" That mayst thou find.   Yet I will place thee
          whence
A way there is : mortals have on it sped;
Ay, and return'd thereby : so let us hence."
Then swift to earth her willing prey she bore,
And left her on the wide Laconian shore,
Alone, at midnight, in the darkness dense.

13

'Twas winter; and as shivering Psyche sat
Waiting for morn, she question'd in her mind
What place the goddess meant, arrived whereat
She might descend to hell, or how should find
The way which Gods to living men deny.
"No Orpheus, nay, nor Hercules am I,"
Said she, "to loosen where the great Gods bind."

14

And when at length the long-delaying dawn
Broke on the peaks of huge Taÿgetus,
And Psyche through the skirts of dark withdrawn
Look'd on that promontory mountainous,
And saw high-crested Taleton in snow,
Her heart sank, and she wept with head bent low
The malice of her foe dispiteous.

15

And seeing near at hand an ancient tower,
Deserted now, but once a hold of men,
She came thereto, and, though 'twas all her power,

Mounted its steep unbroken stair again.
"Surely," she said, for now a second time
She thought to die—"this little height I climb
Will prove my shortest road to Pluto's den.

16

"Hence must I come to Tartarus; once there
Turn as I may," and straight to death had sprung;
When in the mossy tower the imprison'd air
Was shaken, and its hoary stones gave tongue,
"Stand firm! stand firm!" that rugged voice out-
       cried;
"Of such as choose despondency for guide
Hast thou not heard what bitterest fate is sung?

17

"Hearken; for I the road and means can teach
How thou mayst come to hell and yet escape.
And first must thou, that upper gate to reach,
Along these seagirt hills thy journey shape,
To where the land in sea dips furthest South
At Tænarus and Hades' earthly mouth,
Hard by Poseidon's temple at the cape.

18

"Thereby may one descend: but they that make
That passage down must go provided well.
So take in either hand a honey-cake
Of pearlèd barley mix'd with hydromel;
And in thy mouth two doits, first having bound
The pyx beneath thy robe enwrap'd around:
Thus set thou forth; and mark what more I tell.

19

"When thou hast gone alone some half thy road
Thou wilt o'ertake a lame outwearied ass;
And one that beats him, tottering 'neath his load
Of loosely bundl'd wood, will cry *Alas;
Help me, kind friend, my faggots to adjust!*
But thou that silly cripple's words mistrust;
'Tis planted for thy death.   Note it and pass.

20

"And when thy road the Stygian river joins,
Where woolly Charon ferries o'er the dead,
He will demand his fare: one of thy coins

Force with thy tongue between thy teeth, thy head
Offering instead of hand to give the doit.
His fingers in this custom are adroit,
And thine must not set down the barleybread.

21

"Then in his crazy bark as, ferrying o'er
The stream, thou sittest, one that seems to float
Rather than swim, midway 'twixt shore and shore,
Will stretch his fleshless hand upon the boat,
And beg thee of thy pity take him in.
Shut thy soft ear unto his clamour thin,
Nor for a phantom deed thyself devote.

22

"Next, on the further bank when thou art stept,
Three wizen'd women weaving at the woof
Will stop, and pray thee in their art adept
To free their tangl'd threads.   Hold thou aloof;
For this and other traps thy foe hath plan'd
To make thee drop the cakes out of thy hand,
Putting thy prudence to perpetual proof.

23

"For by one cake thou comest into Hell,
And by one cake departest; since the hound
That guards the gate is ever pleasèd well
To taste man's meal, or sweeten'd grain unground
Cast him a cake; for that thou mayst go free
Even to the mansion of Persephonè,
Withouten stay or peril, safe and sound.

24

"She will receive thee kindly; thou decline
Her courtesies, and make the floor thy seat;
Refusing all is offer'd, food or wine;
Save only beg a crust of bread to eat.
Then tell thy mission, and her present take;
Which when thou hast, set forth with pyx and cake,
One in each hand, while yet thou mayst retreat.

25

"Giving thy second cake to Cerberus,
The coin to Charon, and that way whereby
Thou camest following, thou comest thus

To see again the starry choir on high.
But guard thou well the pyx, nor once uplift
The lid to look on Persephassa's gift;
Else 'tis in vain I bid thee now not die."

26

Then Psyche thank'd the tower, and stoopt her
    mouth
To kiss the stones upon his rampart hoary;
And coming down his stair went hasting south,
Along the steep Tænarian promontory:
And found the cave and temple by the cape,
And took the cakes and coins, and made escape
Beneath the earth, according to his story.

27

And overtook the ass, but lent no aid;
And offer'd Charon with her teeth his fee;
And pass'd the floating ghost, in vain who pray'd;
And turned her back upon the weavers three:
And threw the cake he loved to that hell-hound
Three-headed Cerberus; and safe and sound,
Came to the mansion of Persephonè.

28

Kindly received she courtesy declined;
Sat on the ground; ate not, save where she lay
A crust of bread; reveal'd the goddess' mind;
The gift took; and return'd upon her way:
Gave Cerberus his cake, Charon his fare,
And saw through Hell's mouth to the purple air
And one by one the keen stars melt in day.

29

Awhile from so long journeying in the shades
Resting at Tænarus she came to know
How, on the eastern coast, some forty stades,
There stood a temple of her goddess foe.
There would she make her offering, there reclaim
The prize, which now 'twas happiness to name,
The joy that should redeem all passèd woe.

30

And wending by the sunny shore at noon,
She with her pyx, and wondering what it hid,
Of what kind, what the fashion of the boon

She carried, but to look on was forbid,—
Alas for Innocence so hard to teach!—
At fancy's prick she sat her on the beach,
And to content desire lifted the lid.

31

She saw within nothing: But o'er her sight
That looked on nothing gan a darkness creep.
A cloudy poison, mix'd of Stygian night,
Rapt her to deadly and infernal sleep.
Backward she fell, like one when all is o'er,
And lay outstretch'd, as lies upon the shore
A drown'd corpse cast up by the murmuring deep.

FEBRUARY

1

WHILE Eros in his chamber hid his tears,
    Mourning the loss of Psyche and her fate,
The rumour of her safety reacht his ears
And how she came to Aphrodite's gate:
Whereat with hope return'd his hardihood,
And secretly he purposed while he coud
Himself to save her from the goddess' hate.

2

Then learning what he might and guessing more,
His ready wit came soon to understand
The journey to the far Laconian shore;
Whither to fly and seek his love he plan'd:
And making good escape in dark of night,
Ere the sun crost his true meridian flight
He by Teuthronè struck the southern strand.

3

There as it chanct he found that snowy bird
Of Crete, that late made mischief with his queen,
And now along the cliffs with wings unstir'd
Sail'd, and that morn had cross'd the sea between:
Whom as he past he hail'd, and question'd thus,
" O snowy gull, if thou from Tænarus
Be come, say, hast thou there my Psyche seen?"

4

The gull replied "Thy Psyche have I seen;
Walking beside the sea she joy'th to bear
A pyx of dark obsidian's rarest green,
Wherein she gazeth on her features fair.
She is not hence by now six miles at most."
Then Eros bade him speed, and down the coast
Held on his passage through the buoyant air.

5

With eager eye he search'd the salty marge
Boding all mischief from his mother's glee;
And wondering of her wiles, and what the charge

Shut in the dark obsidian pyx might be.
And lo! at last, outstretch'd beside the rocks,
Psyche as lifeless; and the open box
Laid with the weedy refuse of the sea.

6

He guess'd all, flew down, and beside her knelt,
With both his hands stroking her temples wan;
And for the poison with his fingers felt,
And drew it gently from her; and anon
She slowly from those Stygian fumes was freed;
Which he with magic handling and good heed
Replaced in pyx, and shut the lid thereon.

7

"O Psyche," thus, and kissing her he cried,
"O simple-hearted Psyche, once again
Hast thou thy foolish longing gratified,
A second time hath prying been thy bane.
But lo! I, love, am come, for I am thine:
Nor ever more shall any fate malign,
Or spite of goddess smite our love in twain.

8

" Let now that I have saved thee twice outweigh
The once that I deserted thee : and thou
Hast much obey'd for once to disobey,
And wilt no more my bidding disallow.
Take up thy pyx ; to Aphrodite go,
And claim the promise of thy mighty foe ;
Maybe that she will grant it to thee now.

9

"If she should yet refuse, despair not yet ! "
Then Psyche, when she felt his arms restore
Their old embrace, and as their bodies met,
Knew the great joy that grief is pardon'd for ;
And how it doth first ecstasy excel,
When love well-known, long-lost, and mournèd well
In long days of no hope, comes home once more.

10

But Eros leaping up with purpose keen
Into the air, as only love can fly,
Bore her to heaven, and setting her unseen

At Aphrodite's golden gate,—whereby
They came as night was close on twilight dim,—
There left, and bidding her say nought of him,
Went onward to the house of Zeus most high.

11

Where winning audience of the heavenly sire,
Who well disposed to him was used to be,
He told the story of his strong desire;
And boldly begg'd that Zeus would grant his plea,
That he might have sweet Psyche for his wife,
And she be dower'd with immortal life,
Since she was worthy, by his firm decree.

12

And great Zeus smiled; and at the smile of Zeus
All heaven was glad, and on the earth below
Was calm and peace awhile and sorrow's truce:
The sun shone forth and smote the winter snow,
The flowĕrs sprang, the birds gan sing and pair,
And mortals, as they drew the brighten'd air
Marvel'd, and quite forgot their common woe.

13

Yet gave the Thunderer not his full consent
Without some words: "At length is come the day,"
Thus spake he, "when for all thy youth misspent,
Thy mischief-making and thy wanton play
Thou art upgrown to taste the sweet and sour:
Good shall it work upon thee: from this hour
Look we for better things.   And this I say,

14

"That since thy birth, which all we took for bliss,
Thou hast but mock'd us; and no less on me
Hast brought disfavour and contempt ywiss,
Than others that have had to do with thee:
Till only such as vow'd themselves aloof
From thee and thine were held in good aproof;
And few there were, who thus of shame went free.

15

"That punishment is shapen as reward
Is like thy fortune: but our good estate
We honour, while we sit to be adored:

And thus 'twas written in the book of Fate.
Not for thy pleasure, but the general weal
Grant I the grace for which thou here dost kneel;
And that which I determine shall not wait."

16

So wingèd Hermes through the heaven he sped,
To warn the high celestials to his hall,
Where they should Psyche see with Eros wed,
And keep the day with feast ambrosial.
And Hermes, flying through the skiey ways
Of high Olympus, spread sweet Psyche's praise,
And bade the mighty gods obey his call.

17

Then all the Kronian gods and goddesses
Assembl'd at his cry,—and now 'twas known
Why Zeus had smiled,—the lesser majesties
Attending them before his royal throne.
Athena, mistress good of them that know,
Came, and Apollo, warder off of woe,
Who had to Psyche's sire her fate foreshown;

M

18

Demeter, giver of the golden corn,
Fair Hebe, honour'd at her Attic shrine,
And Artemis with hunting spear and horn,
And Dionysos, planter of the vine
With old Poseidon from the barren sea, .
And Leto, and the lame Hephæstos, he
Himself who built those halls with skill divine. .

19

And ruddy Pan with many a quip and quirk
Air'd 'mong those lofty gods his mirth illbred,
Bearing a mighty bowl of cretan work:
Stern Arês, with his crisp hair helmeted,
Came, and retirèd Hestia, and the god
Hermes, with wingèd cap and ribbon'd rod,
By whom the company was heralded.

20

And Hera sat by Zeus, and all around
The Muses, that of learning make their choice;
Who, when Apollo struck his strings to sound,

Sang in alternate music with sweet voice:
And righteous Themis, and the Graces three
Ushering the anger'd Aphrodite; she
Alone of all were there might not rejoice.

21

But ere they sat to feast, Zeus bade them fill
The cup ambrosial of immortal life,
And said "If Psyche drink,—and 'tis my will,—
There is an end of this unhappy strife.
Nor can the goddess, whose mislike had birth
From too great honour paid the bride on earth,
Forbid her any more for Eros' wife."

22

Then Aphrodite said "So let it be."
And Psyche was brought in, with such a flush
Of joy upon her face, as there to see
Was fairer to love's eye than beauty's blush.
And then she drank the eternal wine, whose draught
Can Terror cease: which flesh hath never quafft,
Nor doth it flow from grape that mortals crush.

23

And next stood Eros forth, and took her hand,
And kisst her happy face before them all :
And Zeus proclaim'd them married, and outban'd
From heaven whoever should that word miscall.
And then all sat to feast, and one by one
Pledged Psyche ere they drank and cried *Well done!*
And merry laughter rang throughout the hall.

24

So thus was Eros unto Psyche wed,
The heavenly bridegroom to his earthly bride,
Who won his love, in simple maidenhead :
And by her love herself she glorified,
And him from wanton wildness disinclined ;
Since in his love for her he came to find
A joy unknown through all Olympus wide.

25

And Psyche for her fall was quite forgiven,
Since 'gainst herself when tempted to rebel,
By others' malice on her ruin driven,

Only of sweet simplicity she fell :—
Wherein who fall may fall unto the skies ;—
And being foolish she was yet most wise,
And took her trials patiently and well.

26

And Aphrodite since her full defeat
Is kinder and less jealous than before,
And smiling on them both, calls Psyche sweet;
But thinks her son less manly than of yore :
Though still she holds his arm of some renown,
When he goes smiting mortals up and down,
Piercing their marrow with his weapons sore.

27

So now in steadfast love and happy state
They hold for aye their mansion in the sky,
And send down heavenly peace on those who mate,
In virgin love, to find their joy thereby :
Whom gently Eros shooteth, and apart
Keepeth for them from all his sheaf that dart
Which Psyche in his chamber pickt to try.

28

Now in that same month Psyche bare a child,
Who straight in heaven was namèd Hedonè
In mortal tongues by other letters styled;
Whom all to love, however named, agree:
Whom in our noble English JOY we call,
And honour them among us most of all,
Whose happy children are as fair as she.

29

ENVOY

IT IS MY PRAYER THAT SHE MAY SMILE ON ALL
WHO READ MY TALE AS SHE HATH SMILED ON ME.

NOTE

NOTE

On the Spelling

SINCE many readers will probably remark the spelling of this poem, I will give some explanation of it, so as to escape, if I may, from the reproach of mere peculiarity. The poem being a narrative,— and it is little more than a translation of Apuleius' tale,—the past tenses and participles of verbs occur very frequently, and these being in the common spelling overloaded with mute letters, I saw that it would much lighten the look of the verse to spell them as they are often spelt, and have been spelt from the first, in a shortened form, as they are pronounced.

The first rule seemed to be never to admit any mute letter which was not in the present tense. Thus while *name* makes *named*, *maim* makes *maim'd*, the apostrophe being a concession to common use. With regard to words which have their perfect tense sometimes spelt with a *t*, as *kissed*, which in many books appears as *kist*, these are really pronounced with *d* or *t* according to the sound which happens to follow them : thus they take *d* before a vowel or soft *th*, but *t* before an aspirate or a pause. The apparent inconsistency in the text is due to observation of the actual pronunciation. As to words like *wrinkled*, which is here spelt *wrinkl'd*, this spelling will be quite familiar when "Paradise Lost" is printed as Milton wrote it, which is now the general desire of those who may expect to have their opinion respected : *l'd* is the best spelling, because the *e* is not pronounced (it must give *led* or *eld*), the *l* being a semi-vowel in this position. It struck me that Milton's use of the short spelling might have been due partly to the very consideration which led me to adopt it, that is, that he may have wished to lighten the appearance of his lines, in which preterites are frequent from the like cause as they are in mine : and when I discovered reason for spelling the same words differently (as *kiss'd* and *kist*), I thought that I might have hit on the key to his inconsistencies, but this did not prove to be so.

I have also omitted the *l* from the word *could*. Everyone will agree that it is a useless intruder, but it may not be so well known that the word was always properly spelt until some way on in the sixteenth century, and that Dryden wrote *cou'd*, and that this protest lasted on nearly to this century ; as may be seen under the word *can* in Dr. Murray's new dictionary. Our newspapers show a really romantic reverence for

N

the present orthography, but it has, I believe, no
authority but that of ignorant or fortuitous convention,
and it might better be called typodæmonography.
Owing to its tyranny the use of any unconventionality
in spelling has of late years been too great a disadvan-
tage to authors for them to venture it, for it would have
distracted the reader's attention and provoked ridicule ;
but now that old books are so much reprinted in
their original form, this only real objection is being
done away with, and I, for one, hope that authors
will gradually dare to spell as they like, and assist
towards a real orthography of our tongue.

Works by Robert Bridges

SHORTER POEMS. Fourth Edition, with the addition of
Book V. for the first time included. Printed on handmade paper. Fcap.
8vo. 5*s.* net.

EDEN: AN ORATORIO. Composed by C. VILLIERS STANFORD.
Words only by R. BRIDGES. Fcap. 8vo, paper wrapper. 2*s.* net.

ACHILLES IN SCYROS. A drama, in a mixed manner.
Uniform with "Shorter Poems." Fcap. 8vo. 2*s.* 6*d.* net.

A SERIES OF PLAYS. Fcap. 4to, printed on handmade
paper, double columns, paper wrappers, each 2*s.* 6*d.* net (except No. 8).
The 8 Plays are paged consecutively, and are intended to form a Volume.

   1. *NERO.* The First Part. History of the first five years of Nero's
     reign : with the murder of Britannicus to the death of Agrippina.
                               [*Out of print at present.*

   2. *PALICIO.* A romantic drama in five acts, in the Elizabethan
     manner.

   3. *THE RETURN OF ULYSSES.* A drama in five acts, in a mixed
     manner.

   4. *THE CHRISTIAN CAPTIVES.* A tragedy in five acts, in a mixed
     manner, without change of scene.

   5. *ACHILLES IN SCYROS.* A drama in five acts, in a mixed manner,
     without change of scene.

   6. *THE HUMOURS OF THE COURT.* A comedy in three acts, in
     the Spanish manner.

   7. *THE FEAST OF BACCHUS.* A comedy in five acts, in the Latin
     manner, without change of scene.

   8. *NERO.* The Second Part. In five acts: comprising the conspiracy
     of Piso to the death of Seneca, in the Elizabethan manner. 3*s.* net,
     with general title-page, &c., for the volume.

LONDON : GEORGE BELL AND SONS

CHISWICK PRESS :—CHARLES WHITTINGHAM AND CO.
TOOKS COURT, CHANCERY LANE, LONDON.